MURDER ON VANCOUVER ISLAND

Hatred, prejudice, or a heinous crime without motive?

KATHY GARTHWAITE

Paperback edition published by

The Book Folks

London, 2019

This book is a work of fiction. Names, characters, businesses, organizations, places and events are either the product of the author's imagination or are used fictitiously. Any resemblance to actual persons, living or dead, events or locales is entirely coincidental. The spelling is British English.

ISBN 978-1-0932-5333-7

www.thebookfolks.com

To Judy W.
For the hours of coffee, dessert, and discussions about books and life.

Chapter 1

It surprised David Hunter to see all the doors were closed. Was he the first one here today? It rarely happened that way. He threw his knapsack on the ground and fumbled about for a key; it was hiding out near the bottom, he was sure. A loud thump sounded somewhere out on the street, distracting him momentarily. When he reached for the handle, the door swung inward a few inches. He pushed on it, but something blocked the motion. A peek inside showed a dark lump on the ground. With every bit of his weight he pressed harder, but the obstruction wouldn't budge. He reached through the gap searching for the light switch with his fingertips. The lone bulb that dangled from the cracked ceiling came on slowly, leaving shadows in the corners. The next glimpse sent him reeling back in horror. A hand, baby soft and smooth with dainty long fingers, was resting on the bottom tread as if the person was trying to clamber up the stairs. Tiny tracks of glistening blood trailed across a body and up the lifeless walls. Blow flies charged around the pokey landing with a nasty buzzing.

"Oh my God," David cried out and twisted away. For a moment his breathing ceased. He peered back inside and recognized the tight bike shorts. As he tried to squeeze through the opening, someone nudged him from behind. He braced himself so as not to step forward onto the body and spun to confront the idiot.

"What the hell!" David scowled and flexed his fists, barely able to restrain himself from decking the fool. He propelled Tim Sanderson away from the door, but not before the guy stole a look.

"Holy shit. Is that who I think it is?"

"Yeah." David pulled out his cell and dialed 911.

"Do something," Tim shouted.

"Like what?"

The sirens started whirring like a ceiling fan on a hot summer day. David looked around as the ambulance closed in speedily down the empty streets of Victoria, BC toward the university. The firepit still glowed from last night, an occasional wisp of smoke escaping the coals. In the distance, the peaks of the Olympic Mountains dusted with an early snowfall glistened. The din grew louder, blasting his eardrums with intermittent pandemonium.

"What are you guys doing?" Jason Marsden, the foreman, demanded as he came round the corner of the building. "Let's get moving."

He placed his palm against David's back to force him forward. But David dug his heels in and remained rooted to the spot like the saplings on the boulevard.

"There's been an accident," he stammered, his nerves jangling. "If you call getting your skull caved in an accident."

"Out of my way," Jason insisted and barged through to the now half-opened door. He turned away quickly and stumbled backward, his tanned complexion blanched a green sickly glow. "Did he fall?" The tremor in his voice rang out.

"Are you kidding?"

The crushing of gravel announced another person racing towards them.

"Hey, what's up?" Nick Jones asked. "Am I late?"

A bitterness crept up David's throat, leaving a sour taste behind his tongue. He faltered and felt the blood flee his face and a chill stalk down the back of his neck. Jason's appearance had mottled into a grey pastiness that matched his flat hair and dull eyes. Tim's normal blow and bluster was replaced with lips puffing in chaotic gasps, although he tried desperately to hide his fear by greeting his buddy with daring.

"Take a look."

Nick reached for the door, but the squawk of a siren stopped him. He peered over his shoulder as a vehicle pulled into the yard. The howling sound ended, but the blue and red lights continued to rebound between the two maintenance buildings.

"Oh, Oh. Trouble," Nick mumbled, glancing at his buddy.

"Wasn't me!" Tim said.

A door slammed, and then another. Two detectives dressed in civilian clothes emerged.

"What's the problem here?" Detective Constable Danny Na asked as he approached the men. His open-neck shirt and pressed pants hung loosely on his svelte frame. If this made him look like someone who could be pushed around, his sharp, brown eyes belied this illusion. He was all business. His partner, Detective Constable Blake Gunner, leaned against the front fender of the police car, his gun hanging idly at his hip. The thin scar on the side of his fleshy face was not something that could be discounted. His lopsided grin was more of a sneer.

"I think Robbie's dead. At the bottom of the stairs." David pointed at the entrance, his hand shaking. He pulled it back to his side embarrassed by his fear.

"What? Spencer?" Nick's eyebrows shot up.

Na seized the handle and opened the door as far as he could. He peered in, swinging his torch around the landing. "Oh boy." With a hint of a frown, he tilted his chin to his partner. "Looks like the guy is dead all right."

Gunner leaned into the vehicle and grabbed the radio phone. "We have a homicide. Get the crime scene unit here."

He listened for a moment, and then replied, "Yes, the inspector. He's on call." The grim twist to his mouth made him look clown-like. "I know. This will choke him. What can do you?"

Chapter 2

Inspector William Gibson had started out early before the indigo skies had warmed to a cyan blue. He had sauntered across the street from his home and wandered down the ramp to a dock that jutted out a hundred yards into the cove. High on the right, a ferry terminal to Mill Bay loomed over him. A quarter-way down, a kayak shop occupied a dazzlingly coloured shack—mustard, plum and fuchsia. The young man who ran the storage and rentals raised his eyebrows as Gibson ambled past toward a triple-layered rack adjoining the shed. He stored his kayak on the middle platform, double-locked and effortlessly accessed. It took ten minutes to set his gear into place, ready for a relaxing tour of the bay.

Soft water caressed the wooden surface as he dipped the paddles from side to side. The kayak glided through the calm. The cry of gulls and the splashing of kingfishers diving for illusive fare were melodious against the background of movement. Boats with their colourful unfurled sails and intricate manoeuvres raced the length of the inlet, putting on a show for spectators on the shore or lounging in the bars and cafés. His muscles worked hard to sustain a constant pace, but the effort kept him warm in the chilly fall air. The day was still early, and he wasn't in a hurry—no work today and his wife, Katherine, was occupied in the greenhouse.

His cell phone buzzed, shattering both tempo and peace. He ceased paddling and looked in the waterproof pack clipped around his midriff for the annoying squeal. Compressing his lips, he grumbled, "Yeah, yeah, I'm coming."

Gibson clenched his jaw, exasperated by the interruption. Dire thoughts invaded his mind. Another day spoiled, but he was uncertain by whom. The job or Katherine? Damn. The office meant disaster had befallen someone—can't be helped—and Katherine meant compromised calm at home, giving him palpitations already. He wasn't positive which scenario was worse, being on call and getting the call or having to soothe his wife. He glanced at the number on the screen.

"Gibson."

"Hi, Inspector. There's been a murder at the university," the dispatcher said, his deadpan voice flat down the line. "Sorry. You need to come in right away."

The news stunned the detective. "Wow! We were at a party there last night. Do you know who the victim is?"

"Robbie Spencer." Fritz rustled the paperwork.

"Has the crime scene unit gone out?" he asked. The name wasn't ringing any bells.

"Yes."

"And Scottie?"

"Yes, Sergeant Cruickshank is on her way."

"Thanks." He hung up, glad his partner was already headed out. For just a moment he tilted his head backward, letting the sunlight fall on his face. Then he dipped the paddles into the water, swung the kayak round and doubled his speed to scoot to the wharf. Katherine would demand an explanation for his hasty departure although she knew the drill. Each time he was on standby and had to take off, her abandonment issues resurfaced. He shivered at the imminent showdown.

Gibson commanded the Vancouver Island Integrated Major Crimes Unit, VIIMCU. He had transferred from Ontario for this much-coveted promotion. Hunting the lowest, the most vile, was his passion. Justice for the victims of hideous crimes drove him forward. He petitioned to be the champion of the underdog, of the sufferer and their families. A rising rage gnawed at his psyche, boiled his blood and threatened to unleash his fury against each despot. And behind all of that, there was a personal reason that he rarely spoke of, not even to his wife.

The kayak bumped the quay—thwack—a little too hard. He hopped out of the boat and whipped a rope around a cleat so he could clear out his gear. With expert deftness, he lifted the boat into its cradle and fastened it with the sturdy straps.

"Until next week," Gibson whispered and tapped the hull. The surface was smooth, reassuring and granted him a modicum of pleasure. He strode up the ramp, past the Seaside Café at the top and crossed the street to his house. Katherine wasn't about, so he stole a hurried glimpse out the kitchen window. She was still in the greenhouse. Her gardens bedded for the winter were barren, but he could see the green of herbs through the glass. She appeared jaunty in the vivid red top and stylish jeans, her hair pulled into a loose ponytail. The lightness of her movements reflected her inner calm—this was her safe zone.

Gibson headed to the bedroom and changed into his official attire. Not a uniform, always a suit. Today he favoured a worsted wool blue suit with a striped blue and white tie. He liked to set a solid precedent for the officers who worked with him. Coming across as professional and acting professionally was imperative both for morale and their public image. He unfastened a lockbox to retrieve the

40 calibre Smith & Wesson semi-automatic pistol and snatched his badge off the dresser.

The door banged, and Katherine glanced toward the disturbance. Gibson knew his suit would tip her off about his intentions. He watched her pleasant countenance draw into a pout, the lines racing from her mouth setting into a sulk. She twisted to stand facing the other way.

"Turning aside doesn't mean I'm not leaving," Gibson said as he opened the greenhouse door, and the sweet fragrance of basil came tumbling out. He slipped into the heady warmth. "Katherine, you realize I have to go when on call." He spoke in a soothing, placating tone. She remained quiet.

"It has to be something awful for the dispatcher to contact me." Gibson paused. This scenario never got easier. "I know today was special. Andrew and Heather will be there. They'll keep you company." Andrew Thompson was Katherine's brother, and Heather Clark was her best friend. Would that persuade her that all would be well? He waited to see which way her mood would swing.

Katherine edged toward the far corner, somewhat aloof. But with the mention of Heather, her expression had relaxed somewhat. A more or less imperceptible smile passed over her lips. Her mouth opened into a heart-shape, then drew into a straight line as she bit her bottom lip. He felt the weight upon his shoulders lift a tiny bit but kept up the chatter, struggling to get intimate, to caress her, to set her mind at rest.

"Don't worry. I'm not deserting you. Text me. I'll call as soon as possible," he pleaded, covering all the bases. Today's lunch was to mark a significant milestone for his wife—the one-year anniversary of her sister's death.

There was a slight uplifting of her mouth. Resignation. She wiped tears from her sad brown eyes with the back of her hand.

"Okay." Her sweetness shone through. Gibson brushed velvet lips across her salty cheek and escaped.

Chapter 3

David's eyes flickered, but Robbie lying dead on the cold cement floor had burned onto his retinas. Every ropey muscle on his buttock and every bump of his spine were accentuated by the skimpiness of his outfit. His cleated shoes faced upwards with one ankle bent sideways at an awkward angle. David blinked and glanced over to the rack where Robbie's street bike was locked, ready for the ride home. A streamlined helmet was placed casually over the seat. His mind skipped back to Robbie's prone figure, his limbs contorted and hands grasping for safety. Blood splotches on his clothes and pooled underneath him shone glossy in the dull light. Bits of dirty blonde hair were glued to the tip of a bat that had rolled against the wall. Pinkish stuff, maybe brain matter forced out of the wound, glistened in the pall of death. The images had found a place to harbour in David's mind, hard as he might try to shake them. Someone was speaking to him. He nodded, uncertain what they were saying. Bile caught in his throat. Don't be sick, he thought, and stood panicked on wobbly legs.

The four men huddled together in shock as a dozen vehicles slipped down the boulevard that ran through the campus and crammed into the small space between the buildings. Soon there was hardly room to move. A low rumble settled to a gradual hum as the crime scene officers set up their stations. From an unmarked vehicle that had slid into the commotion mostly unnoticed, a tall black woman emerged. She marched straight to the constables standing by the landing. Her steel-blue eyes held a wariness as she scanned the scene. Shortly after, a large cube van drove in, snaking its course through the packed courtyard toward the parking lot. Four black-clad officers exited the vehicle, each one larger than the last. David watched their movements as they opened the rollup rear door and tossed out its cargo onto the ground. It looked like tents, poles and lots of rope.

The ruckus started up again. Men pounded stakes and strung tape until a substantial fortress enclosed the crime scene. The detective in command, the tall dark lady—someone had called her Scottie—shouted orders and requests to her workforce. Despite all the action, the maintenance crew remained paralyzed, their feet frozen to the earth as if a flash freeze had swept through the yard.

"Jackie. Something horrible has happened." David had scurried to a long row of poplars at the entrance of the building. When the spring breeze weaved down the open landscape, their leaves would quiver. Now the branches were stripped bare, exposing the furrows on their bark to the harsh storms coming and giving no shelter to him as he stood aloof from the crowd.

"What? What is it? Tell me," his wife demanded, always fearful of the anger that lived at David's workplace.

"There's been an accident. A murder," he whispered, not wanting to say the word aloud. He heard the intake of her breath over the hum of the connection.

"You're kidding, right?"

"Not kidding. Robbie is dead. Someone bashed his skull."

"Oh my god. How terrible. Why?"

"I don't know anything, but there are cops everywhere."

"Should you tell them?" Jackie asked.

"I'm not sure."

"Be careful."

"Thanks. I'll call you when I get a chance," David said and hung up. Most of the crew had arrived and clung together in packs, wondering, guessing and questioning. What happened? Who is it? Who did it? Why? Nobody knew anything for sure. David struggled to remain calm, looking down at his feet, his hands tucked in the pockets of his work pants. He watched the others twitch and shuffle. It wasn't until the black truck with dark tinted windows pulled into the courtyard, silently and stealthy, that his flesh truly crawled with trepidation. The F150 pickup had no strobes and no sirens. David had a sudden urge to run when the man stepped out of the vehicle.

Gibson's feet hit the gravel with power. His long limbs were straight but not stiff. He carried his height with easy self-confidence. His gun-metal eyes were not unblinking but steady. And he had a quirky smile that flashed and softened his ruggedness. Almost perfect, except for the crook in his nose. His image was deceiving to most, hiding the danger that lay underneath.

Gibson let his face harden—a warning for everyone to look out. A murder was as serious as it got, and he would bulldoze his way through to get the killer. When he marched onto his stage, he willingly embraced the tension, the fear and the guilt. The characters in this tragic drama would be exposed as he opened their lives for all to see. He would pry into their buried secrets and reveal their predatory behaviour. Without compunction, he would collect every detail, hear every sound, tune in to every voice and amass the data in his memory. He had a shrewd capacity to recall specifics. Something stored deep in his mind would leap to the front of his consciousness at the most unlikely moment like a fluorescent lamp powering on—slowly flickering and then enlightenment. As he worked his way through a case, every detail was important until it wasn't. Some would be useless information but some would give him clarity. So his routine of scanning the site from the onset was a fundamental part of the process. The goal was to bring the antagonist to his knees.

Gibson turned in a half circle and squinted in the sunshine as he inspected the scene, his glance roving over the crew. The men stood stationary with lips parted and breathing almost nonexistent. All curiosity had shifted to him. Men of all sizes and shapes clustered near the crime scene, dressed in coveralls, dirty jeans and heavy tops. Most had expressions of disbelief creasing their faces. Some had looks of infinite indifference. He knew the maintenance crew were waiting nervously for the next thing to happen. Was one of these men the murderer? Was it the loner remaining just feet from the circle—a part of the group, yet not? Did he distance himself from the others because of shyness, dislike or something more sinister? Did the two fellows standing close have a pact? Were they best of allies? Or partners in crime? A heavy-set man with a protruding paunch was smoking a cigarette. He stared at the ground. Was he peering into the past? Or the future? They followed Gibson with their eyes as he advanced across the courtyard. Even the ones with downcast eyes observed him, surely sensing he was the real director of this play.

Walking was made difficult by the loose aggregation of water-worn gravel and the array of vans, cruisers and trucks that jammed the yard. Gibson zigzagged his way over to the second in command, Sergeant Ann Scott Cruickshank. She stood close to the crime scene, her hand brushing the bright yellow tape. The black suit and business-like white blouse instilled a sense of sternness while an occasional Cheshire grin flashed and showed her compassion. Often chestnut curls would border her face and soften her toughness, but today she wore her hair in a tight bun. She towered over most men, making her a formidable and significant presence at every investigation. He knew that she would have finished the initial walk-through and secured the location so evidence didn't get destroyed or moved. There were lights set on large stands tucked against the wall, ready to use if the day turned to night. Even though it was early, today and the next few weeks could be long days for all the people involved. He noticed that several police officers were wandering through the parking lot with heads bent. Good. The search for clues had already begun. The sergeant looked up as Gibson walked toward her.

"Hi, Billy," she addressed her boss, giving him a fleeting flash of her grin. Thank goodness none of the other officers dared to use her pet name for him. Not to his face anyway.

"Hi, Scottie," he shot back. It was a nickname she had been given early in her career, and it had stuck.

The two detectives stood opposite and spoke softly while they waited for the medical examiner. Scottie gave him a brief account of everything she knew so far—nothing really. As they discussed their strategy, the crime unit team carried on with their tasks. Flashes of light from a camera inside the canopy competed with lights still blinking from police vehicles. The photographer was taking pictures of the body and the blood spatter from every angle. At one point, Gibson saw him swivel and snap off a roll of the maintenance crew hanging out by the garage doors. The photographer deposited his camera into a bag and hauled out a video cam. Positioned in front of Robbie, he spun around once again but this time capturing the point of view of the victim.

The medical examiner arrived with a screeching halt on the loose gravel, his standard grand entrance. The door slammed shut, and Dr. Rod McNeill stood indifferently, anchoring a hand on his hip. His shaggy, dark hair with flecks of white at the temple bestowed a distinguished

English gentleman's appearance. Although Rod was a short man, his well-fitted suit transformed his brawny build into a flattering natural V shape. Nodding in their direction, he strolled over to them, a dark leather briefcase tucked to his side. He swept up the tape with a hand sporting neatly trimmed nails and a French polish, and scooted under. The detectives followed.

Gibson looked at blood spatter on the wall and the metallic silver powder dusted all around. Straight ahead was a flight of narrow stairs and to the left a door that lead to the garage. The landing was too small for three people and a body, so they stood close together, elbows rubbing. A sickly-sweet smell assaulted their nostrils. Scottie bristled slightly at the stench and swatted at the flies that tried to alight on her face. Nothing bothered Rod so he got down to business at once. He placed his case on the floor, took out several pairs of latex gloves and handed a pair to both detectives to ensure no cross-contamination.

Nobody spoke while Rod readied himself. He tugged on his trousers and knelt down on his right knee. Then he laid two gloved fingers on the victim's neck looking for a pulse. He had told Gibson a long time ago that this was a well-advised routine as he had been surprised before—never good. He looked at his watch, declared Robbie dead and marked the time in his book, pressing his lips together—neither smiling nor frowning. Some men had inched closer to the yellow tape, curious to view the proceedings. They pushed hard against the line that protected the crime scene. Others had shrunk away from the grisly sight.

"Could you help me with this?" Rod asked, turning to the inspector. "Face him up."

"Oh, sure." Gibson's knee cracked as he lowered himself next to the body. But got no comeback, no chuckles or banter. Not here, not now.

They unbuckled the straps of the backpack hanging from Robbie's arms and put the bag aside. Rod grabbed the shirt at the shoulder while Gibson seized the shorts. Because of the space limitations, they had to rotate the corpse away from them. On the count of three, they heaved, grunted and tugged the man onto his back. Scottie knelt down on the other side, ready to stop the body from getting away from them. A loud thump sounded on the cement as Robbie's head hit the floor. His hazel eyes were wide open and held a desolate sadness, staring past the dingy ceiling to infinity. Dirt and bits of gravel stuck into the skin of his palms and knees. Blood had gushed from the wound and pasted wispy locks of fine hair to his cheeks. Gibson reached out to shut the unseeing eyes but halted with his hand hovering over the face. A silent okay from the ME and he brushed his palm gently over the eyelids. Rod rummaged through his bag and yanked out a pencil. Without disturbing the area exposed by moving the body, he stretched over and prodded at an object tucked in an armpit.

"Well, well, look at this," Rod mumbled as he dragged the wrapped condom from its hiding spot.

A sharp intake of breath broke the silence. Gibson turned quickly to see a man with a hand clasped over his mouth. His eyes were popped open, and his eyebrows raised in a look of fright. Scottie shook her head in dismay and mouthed, "Oh, shit. Complications."

"I'll get my report to you after the autopsy," Rod said as Gibson returned his attention to the ME.

"Tomorrow?" he asked and then added. "Can you give me a time of death?"

"Yes. As I was saying, tomorrow." Rod tilted his head to the ceiling. "To the question of time of death, I can give you an estimate now." He tugged at his sleeve and looked at his watch. "Let's say between five and seven this morning. But don't hold me to that until after the autopsy."

“Okay. Could you give it top priority?” Gibson asked, figuring this new evidence would put a wrench in their investigation.

“I could do that.” Rod plucked off his gloves and threw them in the open bag. He snapped it shut, grabbed the handles and pushed himself to his feet. With a final check around the landing and over to the body, he left the confined space. He departed with a scattering of gravel and a squeal of tires on the asphalt as he hit the boulevard.

Gibson rifled through the backpack before calling over a CSI technician. Both the pack and the condom were placed in evidence bags and tagged. As the technician finished up, the photographer who was hovering nearby, returned to take more pictures without being asked. There was only one thing left to do here. Gibson glanced toward a rumpled looking attendant leaning on a windowless truck, a cigarette hanging from the side of his mouth. A second man leaned against the hood next to him, sucking on a candy. As he walked over, the man pinched the lit end to extinguish it and inserted it in his pocket.

“We’re ready for you.”

“You bet.”

The technicians didn’t waste any time. They had been standing by idly for hours and were happy to get moving. From the back of their truck, they grabbed some equipment and headed over to the landing. They wrapped the body in a white cotton cloth, placed him in a vinyl bag and loaded all onto a stretcher. With their cargo tucked in the back, the technicians jumped into their wagon and spun out of the yard. It was the last time Robbie would leave his workplace.

Chapter 4

An air of melancholy surrounded Gibson as he watched Robbie make his last journey. A hundred orange and yellow lanterns swayed on makeshift wires, and ghostly sheets in the branches fluttered as the wind blew between the buildings. Faint hints of smoke and scorched pumpkins intermingled with the sea mist hanging close to the ground. His breath stuttered from short, shallow bursts to deeper puffs in the chilly air. He glanced at the many technicians dressed in white coveralls darting here and there, busy with their work. To his left, a single storey building sheathed in steel panels made a twanging noise when the wind picked up speed. From the open door, he could see an enormous workshop and tons of tools. The garage door of the two-storey building on his right where the murder had taken place was partially open, pumping out heat into the cold. The sun had fled behind low clouds, casting long shadows on the graveled yard. He remained rooted to the spot as he considered the implications of the condom. It was going to make things difficult that was for sure, but that wouldn't stop him. He would take all the pieces and shuffle them until the puzzle made a clear picture and the murderer was caught.

“What’s our next move?” Scottie asked as she sidled up next to him.

His reflections were cut short like a boat broken loose and drifting to shore. With the whiff of sea air still in his nostrils, he shook himself back to reality.

“We need someone to canvas the neighbourhood.”

“How about Na and Gunner,” Scottie suggested. “I have them with the uniforms in the parking lot.”

“Tell them to check every house around here. Anybody who saw a strange vehicle. Somebody walking around early this morning. The usual.” He turned away for a moment. “Is there another entrance to the building? At the back?”

“I’ll find out.” Scottie scribbled the request on her to-do list and headed to the rear of the building. A two-metre conifer hedge marked the boundary of the yard. Its prickly needles trimmed tight left no room to squeeze through to the other side. Definitely not an escape route. One of the DCs shuffled along the front of it with his head down, searching for any minute trace of evidence. It was a thankless job with a low percentage of results, but had to be done nevertheless. One never knew what would turn up—a footprint, a tossed cigarette or a carelessly dropped ID card. It happened.

“Na. Where’s Gunner?” Scottie shouted, waving a hand to catch his attention.

“He’s back there somewhere.” Na pointed to the corner of the yard as the misplaced DC materialized from behind the hedge.

“Hey, Scottie. What’s up?” Gunner asked. His unruly mess of chocolate hair was covered in dirt and pieces of broken twigs. He brushed his palms across his forehead and flipped the long bangs away from his face.

“Did either of you find anything?”

“Not me,” Na replied.

“Nothing at the back,” Gunner said, his lopsided grin revealing straight white teeth.

"Okay. Let the uniforms finish up here. I have a better job for both of you."

"Whatever you want," Na said.

"The neighbourhood needs to be canvassed. You know the drill. I can count on you. Right?"

"You bet," Gunner replied, happy to be bumped up to a less tedious task. Everybody knew knocking on doors was better than scouring for clues in the dirt. He flipped his hair once again, letting loose a cloud of debris.

"Check houses and apartments in a three-block radius. And the park," Scottie said, giving a sly smile. Undoubtedly, the unspoken word really meant: rouse the homeless camp while you're at it. The guys knew. She didn't have to spell it out. The police ignored the men languishing there as long as there was no trouble. "Oh yeah. The victim didn't have cash or a pocketbook. Maybe it was stolen. Check for that too."

The air had cooled down substantially as clouds had floated in all morning, threatening showers. The workers had drifted to the garage to warm up and gossip. A drone of voices rose and fell with the wind. Gibson followed the buzz. Someone had pushed the steel doors a metre off the ground, making a narrow opening for entry. He stooped over at the waist and slipped inside, giving a suitable grunt as a twinge rapped on his spine. The tables were still set up from the evening before, leaving scant space for the crew. They had squeezed together into groups. Only one guy stood alone, leaning against an old Zamboni which took up most of the floor space. Assorted tools vital for maintaining the university's rink located across the boulevard hung on hooks in the wall or were placed haphazardly on shelves. Gibson heard some snickering and joking interweave through the low hum—a characteristic behaviour he had noticed before, even with his staff. Of course, they were muttering about Robbie and, unfortunately, about the condom found at the crime scene. The whole city would know before long.

"Are there any more workers around?" Gibson asked.

"I'll get them," AJ Stone responded. Although he was tall and solidly built, his face was fleshy. Gibson could see the beginnings of a beer belly. Youthfulness had been lost ages ago as the long dark hair woven with grey receded halfway across his skull. His fingertips discoloured by cigarettes were a ghastly yellow-brown.

"What's your name?"

"AJ. I'm the welder."

"Okay, go."

AJ ducked under the garage door and strolled over to the adjacent building.

"Which one of you discovered the body?" A hush fell over the men. They gawked at the guy by the Zamboni. Someone pointed an accusatory finger in his direction.

"Me," David whispered.

Gibson raised his eyebrows in question.

"David Hunter."

"You knew who the victim was right away."

"Yeah."

"How did you know it was Robbie?"

"His biking shorts," David answered. "His ride is out there."

Gibson pulled up on the garage door, but it wouldn't budge. He gave it a little more effort. The door broke free. David leaped away as it slammed against the frame with a crash. The inspector rubbed a spot near his belt at the back, thinking that was a stupid move. He stepped outside into the pale sunlight and headed toward the end of the building, David following reluctantly behind him. There were several bikes in a stand bolted to the wall.

"Which bike is his?"

"The Kona. The black and silver one."

"Thanks."

David scurried back to the safety of the garage. Gibson looked around the yard for his fingerprint technician. He spotted him just a spit away hunched over an open tailgate, busy organizing a case filled with brushes, powders, tape, lift cards and a magnifying glass—everything needed to catch a print. The other bag beside him would contain all the physical evidence already collected. He walked up to the technician and clapped him on the upper arm.

"Have you got time? Could you fingerprint Robbie's bike?"

"No problem." Snatching his tools, the technician walked over to the bike rack. He pulled out a can of black velvet powder and brushed the silver surface in a circular motion until impressions became visible. Then, he took a photo of the prints before lifting them with tape. He stuck each piece of tape onto a print card. On the black surfaces, he used the metallic silver powder. After finishing, the technician faced Gibson, "Anything else?"

"That's great. Thanks."

"I'll get the results asap. I'll call you." The technician wandered back to his truck and finished packing his equipment into the trunk, all in their appointed cubbyholes.

Some time had passed so Gibson beelined his way back to the garage. The crunching of gravel under his boots would alert the men to someone's arrival. When he appeared in the doorway, their voices swelled from a murmur to a light chatter. More faces had appeared in the crowd. He figured these were the men from the other building.

Scottie was leaning against the wall, scribbling in her notebook. She motioned him with her chin and pointed to an exit at the rear. "Take a gander," she said, and tucked her book into a jacket pocket.

The detectives let the door slip behind them, closing off the gawps and gossip. Scottie indicated some steps leading to the second floor. The wooden stairs were attached to the wall of the steel-clad building but nonetheless looked rickety. Some of the bolts looked loose. Without hesitation, Gibson climbed to the top landing, the stairs swaying with his weight. He pressed down on the long metal handle, and the door lurched open with a thud against the cladding. The spring mechanism that should have stopped the door from hitting the building dangled from a broken bracket. He stepped into a dimly lit hallway. A single bulb hung from its wire, barely giving any light to the narrow space. He walked to the end of the corridor and peered down the stairs to the crime scene. Then he swung around and headed back the way he had come.

"Okay. Two ways in. Two ways out."

"Could be important," Scottie said.

When they returned to the garage, a quietness had fallen. The only noise was an uneasy shuffling and the odd cough as if they were getting ready to watch a movie. Gibson remained in the doorway and surveyed the room. The detectives had worked together for some time now, so Scottie stood calmly and waited for her boss to make the next move.

The baby-faced man who had gasped at the condom chewed nervously on the inside of his mouth. The man looked to be in his forties and had fair, tousled hair and light blue eyes. "I'll start with you." Gibson made eye contact and pointed a finger. "What's your name?"

"What, why me?" he choked. His Adam's apple slid up and down his throat before he answered, "Nick Jones."

"Wait a minute," Jason thundered, taking a stride forward. He puffed out his chest and demanded, "What's going on? You think one of us did this?"

"Jason, right?" Gibson recognized him from the night before. He'd been dressed as a devil, grilling hot dogs on the barbecue.

"Yeah." The foreman's mouth twitched.

"I'll be questioning everyone. I need somewhere private." Gibson's voice had drawn tight with contained irritation. It irked him when someone challenged his authority. He saw Scottie squirm, knowing what she would be thinking—you better watch yourself, pal.

"What the hell!" Jason exploded.

Gibson continued, ignoring the outburst, holding in his impatience. "So where could I set up?" He looked into the coal black eyes and waited some more. He noticed the foreman's uneasy shifting from one foot to the other and kept his stare steady.

After a moment Jason replied, "Use my office upstairs, on the right." He crossed his arms as a sign of cockiness.

Gibson turned to Scottie. "Give me ten minutes. You know what to do."

All the evidence had been collected, and his officers had cleared the crime scene. The maintenance crew would do the cleanup later. Gibson avoided the bloodied landing and headed for the back door, springing up the outside stairs to the second floor. He sensed twenty eyes following his movements. They knew he was a pit bull, he thought smugly. He had their rapt attention now.

Chapter 5

Years of work boots marching in and out of Jason's office had scuffed the grey and white floor tiles. Although the room wasn't large, the place was comfortable. The battered oak desk occupied a considerable chunk of the space. A thin computer monitor with a wireless keyboard dominated the top. Untidy heaps of binders, a wire box filled to overflowing and an enormous jar of pens and coloured pencils obscured the rest. Someone had bumped an ergonomic leather swivel chair against the wall. The two old chairs in front were straight-backed with vinyl seats, stuffing escaping from torn seams. Framed diplomas, a bulletin board and several notices above a narrow bench covered the white walls fading to dismal yellow. A pair of gloves and soiled work boots had been kicked into the corner.

Gibson pulled the plush chair toward the desk and sat down. He shifted the keyboard to the side and placed his notepad and pen in its place. He adjusted the lumbar setting to a comfy position, wiggling into its softness, and leaned back into the silky-smooth material. An abrupt noise startled him, and he glanced up to discover Nick standing in the open doorway, a bashful grin on his face.

With a wave of his hand he indicated for him to sit. Just as Nick perched on the closest seat, a rumble echoed from the hallway, and Katherine came storming into the office. Like the telltale ripples of water revealing where the wind was whistling and where rocks were concealed below the surface, Gibson recognized the signs confronting him now. The perspiration collected above her lip, a glisten on her forehead and the haunted unfocused stare forward were all classic signs and present. She was in a full-blown panic attack. Her eyes were puffy, and tear stains and black mascara had left trails down her flushed cheeks. He could barely hear her flat breathing even in the stillness of the room. She held her shaking hands into a death clutch, unable to control her fear.

"Sit tight. Be right back," Gibson said to Nick as he flew out of his chair. He shifted from behind the desk and approached his wife. He planted his hand lightly on her arm and steered her into the corridor, shutting the door behind them.

"What's going on? Did you drive here in that state?" he asked softly. 'What the hell are you doing here?' was really what he wanted to say.

"State...my state is agitated, not incompetent." She sobbed. "I need you to be there. It's urgent." She leaned into the wall as her limbs wobbled, overwhelmed with dread. She brushed away the dampness from her brow as another wave of doom made her tremble hysterically.

"Katherine, I would rather have lunch with you, but I can't. Not right now. You know that." He wanted to reach out and comfort her. Instead, he raised his palms upwards in defeat. She pleaded with her eyes, swiping at the mess on her satin skin with the back of her hands. The soulful chestnut eyes tipped the scale for him so he placed his arms around her shoulders and drew her in tight. "It'll be fine."

He rubbed her back with consoling strokes.

"But the anniversary is today," Katherine said, tugging away from him.

"We'll meet up later. Get Heather and Andrew to come over tonight." Gibson paused. "We'll honour your sister tonight. Promise."

A tiny flicker of light showed itself in her eyes. He dared a smile, just a small one that wouldn't set her off again. He knew how to calm Katherine during one of her attacks—attacks that arose because of her abusive and bullying ex-husband. Maiming or killing the bastard would satisfy him but being her rock was more important. He burned with rage just thinking about the guy.

Her laboured breathing slowed, almost imperceptible. He soothed her further with his chatter. There was nothing else he could do. At least the noise caused her to concentrate on him and not on her overwhelming apprehension, so he talked.

"A worker was struck early this morning and didn't survive," Gibson said, giving his wife the watered-down version of the savage crime.

Her eyebrows shot up with sympathy.

"I need to talk to everyone while things are fresh in their minds."

She listened keenly, a slight tilt to her head.

He carried on. "Scottie and I will question the workers to see what they know. Na and Gunner are looking for witnesses. Anything suspicious or strange vehicles." Gibson quit speaking and settled his hand under her chin, raising her face to his.

"Long day for you," Katherine said and smiled meekly. "I shouldn't—"

He stopped her by placing his mouth on her swollen lips. She leaned into his sturdy body. A door banged open. They ripped apart. He sensed Nick's baby blues staring at their embrace.

"I'll be right with you," Gibson said, a blush searing through his cheeks.

"Love you," Katherine whispered as she drew away. "See you later then."

He breathed a sigh of relief. She was learning to cope with what can be a debilitating event. He was glad she trusted him—that he would be there for her always. Although Gibson had demons he grappled with—didn't we all—he put Katherine's struggles first. He heard the soft footfalls as she tiptoed down the stairs. He returned to the office and flung himself into the snug chair. Time to launch the interrogation.

Chapter 6

Scottie propped open the door leading to the outside staircase. She snagged a bench, dragging the twenty-two kilo weight to the opening—no sweat. With a small pad in her lap, she was ready to record all the gossiping, the scoffing and the looks. But before undertaking anything, she needed the essentials. She had jotted down Nick's name, address and contact numbers, then told him to head on upstairs. At the exit Nick turned and gave Tim a knowing glance and flipped a salute, suggesting, 'Don't worry. I won't say a word.'

'You better not.' Tim's glare back was palpable. A chaotic echo drummed down to the garage as Nick stumbled on the stairs—once, twice. The crew laughed at his clumsiness.

Scottie was pretty sure those two would lie for each other, especially after watching that little scene between them. Nick had been glued to Tim like honey to a bear. The alpha to the zeta—a common thread in a bully relationship. Tim required a gallery, and Nick needed to feel important because of his vulnerabilities—whatever they were.

Back to the task at hand, Scottie called each crew member separately to obtain their information. They were averse to comply. She had to yank every syllable out of them. Because she was a woman? Possibly? Maybe they were just assholes. She hummed softly, covering her mouth to hide the smirk. She wasn't sure why she did that. They couldn't read her mind.

"Yeah, your cell phone number too."

Tim protested. He stamped his feet and strutted in circles because there was so little space to move. She was undeterred by the men's antics, determining they were testing. Yes, they were definitely assholes. Finally, she had everything recorded in her trusty notebook. She leaned back in her chair, long legs kicked out in front. With a pencil at the ready, she took an all-encompassing glance over the area. Equipment and tools covered every square inch of the cement floor. They had nailed a long 2x4 timber at shoulder height at the rear. A collection of snow shovels and brooms hung on wooden spikes hammered into the wood. There was a ledge above the board packed with different gear. Some of the stuff was foreign to her. A row of metal pegs was screwed into the plasterboard along the last stretch of wall. Down-filled parkas, padded leggings and coveralls were hung carelessly.

The men had spread themselves on the floor or leaned on machinery. Scottie sketched the layout, marking each guy's position on her drawing. She thought this info might come in handy later, perhaps show alliances. She listened to their chatter. No eye contact, no comment. The animosity stunk like a pair of dirty socks. It bounced around the room touching each of them. She tried to make herself invisible to them, but her persona screamed cop. No getting away from it. The men were restless. She watched, wondering if one of them was the killer.

Tim entertained his gallery. He taunted and snorted vociferously, rubbed himself and made obscene gestures. Watching him reminded Scottie of a rooster crowing on top of a chicken coop. A bright red comb crowned the rooster's head announcing his virility. Tim didn't hide behind whispers like the rest of the crew, fearful of the bullying. He was the bully. He spoke loud and salaciously, always nabbing the spotlight.

"Yeah, but those tits. What a lovely sight." Tim cupped both hands, spit spewing from his lips. He glanced around to make sure everybody was watching.

Scottie peered at her notebook.

"Hey, AJ." He prodded at his buddy. "I didn't see your wife last night." Another snigger escaped his abusive lips. Tim's insults had no bounds.

"No. She wasn't there."

"Why's that?" He glared at AJ.

"We're splitting up. I went to the party alone."

"Find some young thing to occupy your time? You, old goat."

AJ laughed. It was better to let Tim mouth off. The alternative could be worse.

Scottie kept her head lowered, but she didn't miss a thing. David had isolated himself from the others. He had been leaning on the Zamboni earlier but had slithered down onto the hard floor. He hunched over his cell, fingers working the keyboard. His blonde hair swept forward, shielding him from the banter. Once in a while, he glanced up at the expletives that spewed from Tim's mouth. In the far corner, Jason whispered to the supervisor from the maintenance building. She glimpsed at her notebook. The pudgy man was Tony. Both of them had angry eyebrows and mouths that twitched. Were they scheming? Getting their stories straight? Scottie thrust the door open wider to let the reek disperse.

* * *

Nick perched on the edge of his chair, a leg crossed over at the knee. One hand rested on his thigh supporting the elbow of his other arm. He stared at a torn seam on his chair.

"Well, Nick Jones. Let's start with last night."

"What? Last night?" A wariness stirred behind his baby blues.

"You let me worry about that. Were you at the party?"

"How do you know about the party?" Nick worked the tear with his finger.

"Well. Yes or no."

"Yes."

"Did you know any of the faculty members that were there?"

"No."

Gibson grew quiet, his eyes down on the desk in front of him. He was sure Andrew had been talking to Nick. Maybe not. He would ask his brother-in-law later.

Nick uncrossed his legs and leaned forward, sliding even closer to the edge of his chair. Soon he would slip right off.

"Does the crew hang out after work?"

"Yeah, sure."

"What kind of stuff are you into?"

"Biking."

"Did Robbie go as well?"

"Sometimes."

Nick bounced in his seat, wanting to break free. He squirmed at the next question.

"Tell me, Nick, why were you surprised when you saw the condom?" He pressed on quickly. "Do you know something?"

"No. Why would I?"

"So the condom didn't mean anything to you?"

"That's crazy." Two bright spots appeared on his cheeks.

Gibson didn't buy it. He thought Nick was holding back. So he leaned forward, pushing his face into Nick's personal space.

"I don't believe you," he said.

"I don't know anything." Nick pressed his lips together.

To keep the secrets from spilling out, Gibson thought. He shuffled the pencil box on the desk, straightened his notebook and pulled back.

"What about baseball? Do you play?"

"No."

"Anybody at work play?"

Nick shrugged.

"What time do you leave for work?"

"Sixty-thirty."

"Do you stop anywhere before you get here?"

"What do you mean?" Nick asked.

"For a coffee or anything?"

"No. I come straight to work."

"Check in with Scottie before you leave." He leaned back further into his chair and crossed his arms.

Nick shot up and left the stuffy room behind.

Gibson heard heavy footfalls as Nick ran down the stairs. His stomach rumbled. He picked up his cell and sent a text. Then he got up to stretch, opened a window and waited to see who Scottie would send up next. The rain had started with a light shower, but the clouds to the south were gathering steam. The university buildings and sports arena across the sodden lawns shimmered through the blanket of drizzle, but he knew that soon a heavy downpour would obscure the view.

* * *

"We need coffee," AJ said. Long hours sitting on cold concrete had frozen his butt. He rubbed vigorously at the muscles to bring them back to life. Fatigue was setting in. He looked haggard, his lips skinny as he gnawed on his cheeks. Almost all the crew were lounging on the floor, restless, tired and hungry.

"And our lunches," Tim shouted.

A thundering sounded as someone came bounding down the stairs. Nick swung around the corner, gasping to catch his breath. It was more from fear than exertion.

"I'm supposed to check in with you."

"You're free to go," Scottie said.

"Talk to you later," Tim yelled.

Nick dashed out the door as quickly as his steel-toed boots would let him, tripping on the metal sill. The garage resonated with a laughter comparable to the heavy braying of a donkey.

"What's the hurry, asshole?" Tim hurled the slur and a finger at the fleeing figure.

"You're up next, David," Scottie said.

He was immersed in his phone and didn't hear the detective.

"David."

"What?" He looked up and brushed a strand of hair behind his ear.

"You can go upstairs now."

"Oh, okay." He stuck the phone in his backpack and skipped out.

Scottie waited for a derogatory remark from Tim.

"Well. What about the food?" Tim asked instead of his usual slander.

"Okay. One at a time."

She looked at her cell when it chirped. 'Need refreshments.'

'Will order sandwiches and coffee.' She texted back.

"My lunch is in the other building," AJ said.

"Go ahead. Just come right back." She didn't want anyone sneaking off.

"What about coffee?" One of the men asked.

"Could you do that, Jason?"

He gave a sneer and stormed out. The stairs rumbled from the force of his boots as he hopped up them two at a time. Scottie stuck her head outside the garage doors, hoping to spot an officer nearby. Luck was with her.

"Could you do me a favour?"

"You bet," Eddy Evans said, a pleasant smile crossing his square face.

Chapter 7

Katherine sat in her vehicle for a few minutes, feeling intoxicated by Gibson's strength. She plopped her head on the back of the seat and bundled her arms around her body, inhaling the smell of his soap, spicy and exotic. The heady scent lingered on her clothing. She closed her eyes and touched her lips, bruised from the passion. A flush warmed her cheeks. Sensing someone was watching, she sat up straight, started the SUV and backed out onto the street. The traffic had thinned from the initial morning rush so she drove the highway at a brisk clip. She took the last off-ramp that bypassed Brentwood Bay proper, missing the bottleneck of the village centre, and shortly pulled into her driveway.

The tune playing on the radio was a favourite so she waited for the song to finish before switching off the engine. She remained subdued, staring off at nothing. Her hands were half-curled into fists. Taking in a quick breath and blowing out slowly was a yoga technique she used more frequently these days. She reached over to the passenger side, snatched her handbag and exited the vehicle. She lumbered down the walkway and unlocked the front door to an empty house. Not totally empty. The trilling of the zebra finches sounded like breakers crashing on a rocky shoreline. She crossed to the living room and the metallic trumpeting song ballooned to a crescendo. She squatted next to the silver-barred cage and whistled an engaging chorus, puckering her mouth and letting the air pass over her tongue. In response, the birds tweeted one more round of their hymn. She placed her coat and handbag on the couch and drifted through to the kitchen.

Katherine glanced at the clock hanging over the sink and realized it was still hours before her lunch date. She had consumed three coffees that morning. The slight tremble in her outstretched hand confirmed that was enough. So she searched the cupboard for a special tea. While she waited for her 'English Breakfast' to brew, she went into the dining room to retrieve her cherished possession. Katherine paused in front of the buffet and opened the frosted glass door. She took out the cup and saucer from the shelf, turning the treasure in her hands, rubbing the deep red flower with her fingertip. 'Country Rose.' A last present from her sister Rose. The threatening tears froze to a lump in her throat. She held her breath, holding back the sense of apprehension that had accompanied her the entire day. An overwhelming sentiment of sadness enveloped her, persisted in her thoughts, in her heart. Her older sister was her rock, and now she was gone. The whole year since she had died felt like a lifetime.

The funeral had been a blur. The clicking of the projector was still trapped in Katherine's ears, sometimes drowning out all sound. Picture after picture of Rose magnified on the screen: as a child, high school graduation, on her wedding day, on holidays, with her family, with Katherine. Then came the condolences, the shaking of hands, the introductions of strangers, and worst, the showdown of estranged relatives. She had stood face-to-face with her younger sibling. Acrimonious was the kindest word she could think to describe the reunion. Her sister had turned aside when she had approached. A slight flip of the hair, a jittery laugh and clacking of heels on tile as Julie had walked the other way. How could they ever make amends? Affection had always been sporadic. 'On again, off again.' Katherine felt abandoned. Not for the first time, her heart skipped a beat. But blood is blood. Should she try again? And what? Feel rejected yet another time?

Katherine pressed the cup to her breast and let out a gigantic sigh. Back in the kitchen, she put her tea and a plate of biscuits on a small tray. A few minutes later she strode out the back door to her sanctuary, clinging to her reflections.

The glass enclosure was set twenty feet down a stone path from the house. The passage, bordered by a perennial garden, bloomed with chromatic variation the whole summer long. Now the beds held only dark brown soil. The richness of the humus rose from the ground as she wandered along the walk. The grass was heavily shaded by woods that edged the periphery. There was no sunlight to peak through the bare branches of the deciduous trees, leaving the backyard dull and dreary. The entire colour came from the conifers. They changed a darker green with a hint of red in the chilly nights. She opened the door to the greenhouse and promptly closed it behind her before the heat escaped. The fan was running full blast, mixing the warmth it generated with the aroma from the herbs growing within. Scents of basil, oregano and chives drifted around her and followed her as she walked down the centre aisle. How intoxicating! Along the outside walls, deep benches stood barren. She turned the radio to a classical music station and hummed as she assessed the pots for moisture.

Over the harmony of the music, Katherine heard the patter of rain on the glass roof. The melodious resonance blended with the violins and brass of one of her favourites. The lullaby evoked images, memories and affections from long ago. Of her youth. Of her ex-husband.

Katherine slumped against the rough bench and looked off into the past.

Arthur Brockelman. The tall and willowy mystic. After all these years, she still pictured his wavy dark hair, smooth skin and olive complexion. He had appeared one day at college and overwhelmed her with his charisma. A whirlwind romance gathered strength as Arthur captured her heart. Katherine glanced at her hands that once stroked his back in the throes of desire. She shuddered at her naivety and clenched her fists. Arthur's true character exposed itself after their hasty marriage. She rubbed at her forehead as the pain threatened to invade her once again. She felt nauseous. The reveal hadn't been pleasant. He had been abusive and cruel.

Katherine gazed over to the drops of rain clinging to the branches of the cherry trees. Akebono—Japanese flowering cherry. This was her favourite tree, giving a dramatic display of fragrant double pink flowers in early spring. The glossy leaves had turned golden yellow and tumbled to the ground only weeks before. Her marriage had started and ended the same.

Arthur's emotional abuse had been scheming, devised to twist her will to his. He maintained absolute power over Katherine. Her school work had faltered when she didn't complete her assignments. He assailed her with quips of women using sexual favours to scale the corporate ladder. 'How else except putting out? What do you know about the workplace anyway?' These derisive remarks that Arthur had flung at her stole her self-esteem and hurt to the core. Still hurt. Finally, she had quit going to classes and lost any hope of achieving her goal of a college diploma. Katherine pushed back the tears as the thoughts looped through and around her.

What had she hoped when Arthur suggested a baby could make them happy? How had she thought everything would be okay? Why did she agree? Because life would become bearable then? Don't make waves, she was told. She had been so confused.

The celebration of becoming pregnant was brief. Only months afterward, Arthur grew more ruthless, a bully. Katherine realized he had dragged her further into their rocky relationship. Then the first panic attack hit. But meaningless compared to what happened next.

A miscarriage!

Katherine sat on a bench to finish her tea. Her body trembled violently. The teacup slipped from her hand and struck the cement floor with a deafening impact. With a glazed stare, she peered at the shattered ruins of the cup. She let out an uncontrollable whimper. Her lips quivered, and tears welled in her eyes. Katherine placed her arms on the counter, rested her forehead in her palms and let the tears flow.

Chapter 8

Gibson didn't raise his head at the sound of approaching footsteps. They were hushed and unobtrusive. But the sharp knock at the door startled him, and he looked up from his notes.

"Hi. Have a seat."

"Okay." David plunked himself in the same place that Nick had just vacated, feeling the warmth left behind. Maybe a little sticky too. From sweat? He perched on the edge of the chair, his stomach knotted up, his feet bouncing off the floor. He cleared his throat twice, clasping and unclasping his weathered hands.

Gibson sat at the desk, bent over in concentration, scribbling in his book. He laid the pen down and angled back. David's mouth was drawn into a straight line, and he was biting his lower lip. David had broad shoulders that rippled with strength. His neck was solid, a thickness that carried down into a husky chest. The muscles of his biceps strained the fabric of his shirt.

"Do you work out?"

That wasn't a question David expected.

"Yeah. There's a gym on campus we can use," he said. He breathed in deeply, thinking this won't be so bad.

The next question came quickly and unexpectedly. “Was Robbie gay?”

“What?” David blew out his breath and looked away. “I don’t think so.”

“So maybe he was?” Gibson had picked up his pen, tapping it softly on the edge of the desk.

“I didn’t say that. That’s not what I meant.” David ran a hand through his hair in a gesture of indecision.

“Is that a yes or a no?”

“No!”

“And the condom. Did that mean anything to you?”

“No,” David repeated, squeezing his eyebrows together and wetting his lips. He shifted his weight, the chair squeaking in protest at his heavy-set frame.

Gibson wasn’t sure David was telling all, so he asked another question to get closer to the truth.

“Robbie was wearing tight shorts and top. That was his usual outfit when he rode, you told me already. What about his work clothes?”

“What?” David gave a quick bark of laughter. His gaze fluttered around the room, never settling on Gibson for long. “Seemed normal.”

“Did he ride his bike every day?”

“A few times a week, I guess. I didn’t pay much attention.”

“Were you a friend? Hang out after work? Play baseball?”

Gibson could see a glisten of sweat appear above David’s lip and his teeth grinding slowly against each other. His face was tanned and his sandy hair was still bleached from the blaring summer sun. The brawny physique, ruddy complexion and mournful hazel eyes didn’t hide his intelligence. Gibson jotted something in his notebook.

“I don’t play baseball.”

Gibson sat silently to let David expose more. It was a common technique for interviewing witnesses. People usually filled the silence with words. It worked.

"We're friends. We did car things together. That's about it."

"What about the bike park? Did you meet up there?"

"Yeah, I suppose."

"Tim. Jason. Nick. Robbie."

David nodded and gave a wry grimace.

"You discovered the body. What were you doing before that?"

"Nothing. Got up. Came to work."

Gibson raised his eyes from his notebook and pressed on.

"You were at the party last night," Gibson stated, not a question. "And saw the fight."

"Yeah, I was there. Saw it."

"What started the fight?"

"Well—"

A shuffling of feet in the hallway made him stop. He turned in his chair. Tim stood in the doorway, his lips curling into a menacing sneer.

"Sorry, just came to get my lunch," Tim said, then pivoted and walked into the lunchroom.

"Go on," Gibson said.

"I don't know what the quarrel was about. Can I leave now?"

"No clue at all?"

David perched himself on the edge of his seat and gave a jerky shake of his head. He glanced around the office before locking his eyes on the detective.

"You can go."

David bounced out of the chair and left the room.

Gibson thought David would be the best person to get the real story about Robbie, but he seemed to be reluctant. He wasn't sure why. They had been friends. He leaned further back into his chair, closed his eyes and reflected on something. Had Tim just threatened David? About what?

Scottie heard soft footfalls on the stairs. David hesitated on the bottom step and then poked his head through the doorway. He glanced around the garage. Tim's bug eyes stared him down. The pulse pounding in David's temples was almost visible. He fled.

"Grasser," Tim shouted.

"You're next, Mr Sanderson," Scottie said.

Tim took his time leaving, an arrogant swagger as he crossed the room. He gave a big thumbs up to AJ, grabbed the door frame and swung himself out. He vaulted up the steps, hitting each tread purposely with all his weight. The stairs vibrated noisily against the steel wall. A bang of the door sent another loud reverberation down the siding. It took a while for the echoing to fade. Gibson opened his eyes, distracted by the racket. It had sounded as if the building was coming down around him. Tim appeared in the doorway, chin held high and hands on hips. He stood unabashedly at the disturbance he had caused.

"Have a seat."

Tim pushed the chair along the tile floor until it was at an angle to the detective. He fell into it, slumped down and sprawled his legs out wide in front of him.

"Just trying to get comfortable."

Gibson stood up and closed the door. He sat back down in his chair and let into Tim immediately.

"What was the fight about?"

"What! Who told you about that?"

Gibson had heard the ear-splitting boom when Tim had pushed Robbie into the wall. Afterward Tim had glared at his opponent with ill intent in his expression and probably his soul.

Gibson didn't reply but watched Tim fume about a possible rat in the group.

"Yeah sure. David's the snitch. That asshole."

"Doesn't matter who. I want to know why."

Tim had passed his thirties a while ago, and yet he still acted the fool. He had ears that stuck out from his undisciplined hair. His sizable forehead was glistening with sweat along his receding hairline. Long blonde lashes flirted with his cornflower-blue eyes. Wrinkles at the corner of his mouth pointed to large pale lips. His complexion darkened from long hours in the sun was pockmarked from teenage acne. Altogether a plain face.

"I don't know. Guess we don't see eye-to-eye. Robbie's such a dweeb." He lowered his chin, biting his nails. "I have nothing to do with that. Really. It wasn't me."

"So the bat's not yours?"

"No!" he shouted. "Don't pin this on me." He jumped out of his seat.

"Sit down. We're not finished," Gibson said firmly.

There was a knock on the door. It opened a crack, and Scottie peeked in. She held up a bag of food in one hand and a coffee in the other. Gibson smiled and waved her forward.

"Thanks."

She placed the package on the desk, gave Tim a smirk and left. Gibson pulled out a hefty-sized sandwich and took a bite. It tasted good. Food always made him feel better. He looked up at Tim and continued munching.

"Tell me about this morning then. What time did you leave for work? Anybody see you?"

"I came straight from home. Sometimes I stop for a coffee, but I didn't today. Got here right after David." He settled back into the chair and crossed his arms over his chest.

"Did the condom mean anything to you?"

"Yeah. Robbie's gay."

"Okay. Did everyone know that?"

"Well, I don't know for sure. He acted gay." There was a big grin hiding behind his words. It showed itself by the twitch at the side of his mouth.

Gibson twirled a pen in his fingers frustrated with the answers he was getting.

"Who else disliked Robbie besides you?"

Gibson smiled in that tense way he did just before he was about to vent. The door swung open interrupting Tim's response. A large paunchy man leaned against the frame. His plump face was pasty with blotches of red up to his balding head.

"Is there a problem?" Gibson asked sharply.

"Yeah, I want this harassment of my men to stop." He tugged at his belt to pull his sloppy pants up higher.

"Okay. You can go, Tim. Come in and have a seat. Tony, right?" He had heard a description of the supervisor. They were right on the money.

Tim launched out of the chair and pushed past Tony to make his escape. There was another slamming of a door. The rumble of the stairs thundered against the building again.

"Tony Sarcone. I have nothing to tell you. My guys were in a safety meeting. We're not involved." He remained in the same spot, his breathing sporadic.

"Not all. David found Robbie," Gibson snapped back.

"Well, my building crew was in the meeting. It was one of those homeless guys. The nutcases." He brandished a hand toward the park. "Nothing to do with us. Period." He punched his finger in the air repeatedly, his voice was shaking.

"We'll talk more about this later."

Tony marched out without another word.

Gibson picked up his coffee and looked out the window again. It was pouring now, hiding the university buildings across the grounds. Did everyone have something to hide here? His brain hurt.

Chapter 9

Andrew was a Professor of Philosophy at the University of Victoria—UVic. to the locals. Philosophy comes from Greek roots, Philo means 'love,' and Sophos means 'wisdom.' A philosopher seeks the meaning of life and the universe. How and why people do things. It is a reflection on everything—to think big thoughts. In reality, he lectured in the mornings and spent afternoons reading and writing. His blog, 'Shattered People,' was a hit with Generation Z.

His office was on the top floor of a building overlooking the sports field. A short corridor led to an elegant waiting room with plush carpeting and soft spot lighting. There was a plethora of colourful animal and bird prints hanging on the walls, showcased by Renaissance nickel art lamps. Today a young lady was busy typing in front of a thin computer monitor. She was dressed in a floppy white knit sweater with cowl neck and black jeans. A carved African motif door with large polished handles and a sign that read 'Welcome' was on her right.

Inside his office, Andrew sat behind the mahogany desk with the overhead lights reflecting off the gleaming surface. Not a paper, pen or file was in sight. The laptop at the side had its lid closed. He leaned back in his ergonomic styled black leather chair and swivelled to look out the window. The sun had been shining earlier, but now the clouds hurried down the Strait of Juan de Fuca to blanket the city with gloom. A brass clock chimed a melodious sound announcing 'time to go.' Andrew turned back toward the room. The timepiece had a special spot on a shelf beside a photo of his two sisters. The bookcase took up a whole wall and extended from floor to ceiling with hundreds of books lined up, row on row. He closed the book on his lap and placed it back in its appointed nook. Then he grabbed his coat, looked around once more and set out for his lunch date. He locked the office door and faced the receptionist with a cheery smile.

"Headed out now. Not sure how long I'll be."

"Okay. See you later. You have an appointment with a student at three." She looked at him over her reading glasses. Her lengthy blonde hair was pulled into a high ponytail and swished as she turned her head. He detected a slight bronze colouring on her eyelids. Her lashes were exceptionally long and her cheeks rosy red. She tapped on the keyboard with pink coloured nails.

"Thanks."

Andrew had chosen her from among several postgraduates who clamoured to get this prodigious job. It was a fast track to coveted permanent positions at the university. She had been setting up appointments and screening visitors for a few months already. So far so good.

He made his way to the faculty parking lot. Sitting on the tarmac was a new Mustang with a polish that reflected the grey sky. Somehow owning this beast and teaching philosophy clashed in the universe. Did he care? He opened the door and slid into the bucket seat. A motor whirred softly and moved the seat to its preset position. He ran his hand along the soft leather. No. He didn't care. The engine roared to life with a throaty sound. He put it into first gear and took the boulevard road out of the university grounds to Cordova Bay Road.

Within fifteen minutes, he was almost at the Sandy Beach Restaurant. It was on the main thoroughfare, so he cruised slowly, scouting for a safe place to park, hoping to avoid door dings. Finally he found the spot he wanted and pulled in. He looked at his watch and realized he was running late. Hurrying, he crossed the road to the restaurant and stepped inside. The panorama view overlooked a pristine bay and stretched on forever on sunny days. Fog hid the farthest landfall now. The beach was filled with logs, blown in by the many fall storms. The yellow sand was soft to walk on and rivalled any California seashore.

Andrew spotted his sister and Heather at once, even in the late lunch crowd. Katherine waved him over. Her pale skin and pink cheeks were China doll beautiful, although all the makeup she had applied didn't disguise her red eyes. Heather wore a plunging neckline dress that swept down her voluptuous figure and finished calf length at her three-inch heels. Her straight, black locks swished as she looked up.

"Hello ladies."

Heather reached out for Andrew's hand. For a moment their fingers touched. A charge of energy ruffled her inscrutable countenance. He remained unaffected and took a seat next to Katherine, looking at the empty chair.

"Gibson's late?"

"He isn't coming. Got called to work," Katherine said. A pained expression crossed her face.

"You're stuck with us. To Rose," Heather said as she raised her drink. No one else picked up a glass so she took a sip of her wine anyway.

"Yes. To Rose," Katherine echoed. She gazed at the floor, zoning in on the ridges and knots of the oak flooring.

Andrew feared his sister was working her way into a lather. Her swollen eyes and harried appearance attested to the fact she was overwhelmed with emotions.

"To Rose," Andrew said. He lifted an empty glass and signalled to the waiter looking their way. The man came over to the table immediately.

"Hi. How is everyone doing today?" he asked, bowing slightly and rubbing his hands together. Andrew saw his sister press her lips tightly as if to stop herself from screaming.

"We're good," Andrew said. "Could I have a drink before we order?" He didn't want to be rude, but the cheerful greeting could set Katherine into another panic attack. The server scurried to the bar.

"I'm here for you. Hope you never forget," Andrew said.

"Me too," piped up Heather. "I am without equal your best friend so let's order. I'm famished." She picked up a menu with a flourish of her hand.

Katherine broke into a smile. It was almost futile to ward off Heather's buoyant grit. The restaurant was renowned for serving local fish. The freshest halibut, lingcod and salmon caught off the west coast of British Columbia were used in exquisite dishes. Combined with local produce and herbs made it nearly impossible to order anything but the fish. And so all three of them did. Each ordered a different entrée so they could sample each other's savoury plate.

"My gallery showing is soon," Heather said, lifting an eyebrow.

"Tell us," Katherine said, sliding her chair closer and leaning in, getting into the spirit.

Heather gave them the details, barely able to hold in her enthusiasm.

"So guys, I expect full compliance attending the show," she said. "No exceptions. I need all the support I can muster."

"Come on. You're famous on the peninsula. People love your work," Andrew said. A few of the prints in his waiting room were original watercolours created by Heather. Three owls sitting together on a conifer branch was his favourite. Owls were solitary creatures but when grouped were called a parliament. They had been known for being wise of disposition. He thought the name was suitable and wonderful.

"Still have to come."

The food arrived quickly. It was great service. They dug in, enjoying the delicious meal. Except Katherine who had slipped back into her bleak mood. She was pushing food around her plate mindlessly. Andrew babbled about his blog in between bites. Heather placed one elbow on the table with her hand under her chin, staring at him as he spoke. She found his clean-shaven face and clear voice irresistible. Not the stereotype at all. He was middle-aged and single. Why didn't he ever ask her out?

"Gibson is investigating a hate crime." Katherine pushed her plate away.

"Oh. What happened? Where?"

"At the university. You didn't hear about it this morning?"

"What! Who got hurt?" Andrew asked.

"Somebody was killed. I'm not sure exactly," Katherine said. "But it was in the maintenance department."

"Oh my god." Andrew's face turned from its usual ruddy complexion to pale in seconds.

"That's all I know."

Heather sat back in her seat, a look of consternation washed over her face.

"Do you need anything else?" The waiter approached the table, the same warm smile looking down on them.

"No. I have to go. Put it on my tab." Andrew bolted out of his chair.

"Where are you going in such a hurry?" Katherine asked.

"The university. I forgot. I have an appointment."

"Oh." Then as an afterthought she asked, "Could you come for drinks tonight? Gibson feels bad he had to miss lunch." She turned to her friend. "You too."

"Yes." Andrew said. He blew his sister a kiss.

"Of course." A huge exhalation of breath escaped from Heather's clamped mouth. She followed Andrew with her eyes as he dashed off and vanished out the door.

Chapter 10

Gibson turned away from the window and the dismal showers. It was only the beginning. The rainy days would stretch from now until March. On the positive side there would also be sunny times that would invite a lark around the bay in his kayak. He smirked at the prospect. A list of all the employees stared up at him. The names of those he had already interviewed had been crossed off. Tony had informed him that the safety meeting ran from five-thirty to six-thirty. That would cross out several more, assuming the murder window Rod gave him didn't change. He put tick marks beside the crew members that had attended the session. That left Jason. Gibson headed down the stairs to expatiate on things. There was still a lot of groundwork to cover today.

"Scottie. Are you making out okay?"

"All good."

"Hey. Can we leave yet?" AJ asked. "We've been hanging out all day."

"Who was at the meeting this morning?"

"Me." Everybody but Jason lifted their arm and called out.

"So nobody heard or saw anything?" Gibson asked.

"No. Nothing." They all shook their heads. Tony stood silently with his arms crossed and eyes narrowed. He was breathing noisily through his mouth.

"Okay. You can all go. I'll chat with each of you alone over the next few days," Gibson said and with a brandish of his hand motioned them to take off. As Jason turned toward the exit with the rest of the gang, Gibson stopped him and said, "Not you. Could you give me a minute?"

Tony stomped out.

"Any word from Na and Gunner?" he asked Scottie.

"Nothing yet."

He turned to Jason and motioned toward the rear door. They headed up the stairs, Jason trailing behind. Gibson stepped over to the desk and sat down. He signalled to the chair in front. Reluctantly Jason sat, adjusting the seat so he faced the detective. He sat up straight, crossed one leg over the other and brought his arms tightly across his chest. His foot jiggled. He had a pinched expression and unwittingly was gnawing the inside of his lip.

"So, you're the foreman here," Gibson said and gestured to the diplomas on the wall.

"Yeah. I worked my way up."

"Did you start as a maintenance guy?" Gibson asked, keeping the conversation light and pleasant.

"No. I was somewhere else before." The corners of his mouth shot up into a grin.

Gibson wasn't sure if it was a sincere smile.

"You're in charge of the ice rink?"

"Yeah. The sports arena, too."

"What time do you start?"

"Seven."

"You did the grilling at the party," Gibson said. "Did you stay behind to clean up?"

"Yup."

"Who else stayed?"

"Tammy. My wife."

Gibson already knew that.

"Anybody else stay?"

"Nick locked up." Jason crossed and uncrossed his arms, smile looking forced now.

"And what about this morning? Did you come straight from home?"

"I went to Best Of Coffee first." After a short pause he added, "I do every morning."

"Someone can verify that?"

"Sure," Jason said.

"Would you say Robbie was a well-liked guy?"

"He got along with everyone. He organized events. We all got along."

"Except for the scrap last night?" Gibson squinted his eyes and peered into Jason's flat grey eyes.

"Things happen," Jason said, breathing in deeply.

"It wasn't a homophobic thing then?" Gibson shot back. He liked to infuse some static into his interviews.

"No. What would give you that idea?" Jason retorted defensively.

"The condom."

That stopped Jason in his tracks. After a few minutes of stillness, he lifted his shoulders but made no comment. Gibson let that go.

"Some of you guys bike together. What about baseball?"

"I don't play. Don't know about anybody else." Jason uncrossed his legs and leaned forward. "Never saw that bat before. If that's what you're thinking."

"That's all for now. Thanks Jason."

"For now?"

"We'll have further questions as the investigation continues."

"Really? I don't see how anyone of us could be involved." He stood up and placed his palms flat on the desk.

"We're going to look around. In both buildings. Okay with you?" Gibson brushed lint from his sleeve.

"Sure."

"Could you show me which locker is Robbie's?"

Jason headed to the lunchroom. Along one wall was a long row of lockers—some with banners and some with names. He tapped on a blue cabinet in the middle with a picture of a muscle car taped to the front and no lock. Gibson reached for the handle. A light jiggle upwards released the door, and it swung open effortlessly. Anybody could have a peek. Or take something. Even put something there. He gazed up and down the row. Only a few didn't have locks.

"I'll be at my desk if you need anything."

Gibson nodded a thanks. He was already examining the contents and recording them in his notebook. The foreman hung around for a few moments, hovering close by. Then he turned and went back to his office, closing the door behind him.

Gibson rooted through the locker, methodically inspecting each item. There was a coat and a pair of lined pants hanging on a large hook. On the top storage rack, there were several automobile magazines, a newspaper from a few days ago and some application forms from local colleges. There was a coffee mug that had known better times with a faded picture of a dog on the front. At the foot of the locker were steel-toed boots and a few stinky socks. Gibson found nothing of significance and placed his pad back in his pocket. He took a perfunctory glance around the room. There was the usual beat-up table and chairs expected in a workplace setting. On the countertop stood a stained coffee maker, a kettle and a microwave.

He scrutinized a drawer that was loaded with a haphazard selection of flatware, an opener and several dull knives. The overhead cupboard had spotted glasses, cracked mugs and assorted plates. Two doors were closed on the far wall. He opened the first one to discover it was a closet with brooms, buckets and cleaning fluids. The other led to a grimy bathroom. The last person hadn't flushed the toilet, giving off an acrid stench. Paper towels were scattered on the mud-covered floor. The sink was filthy. He guessed they didn't use the provisions in the supply closet. All-in-all he found nothing he didn't expect until he glanced in the garbage bin. Downstairs he encountered his partner rifling through the sideboards. She had walked around the area examining every nook and cranny. Lots of machinery, work gear and parkas filled the room.

"Anything out of the ordinary?" Gibson asked.

"No. You?"

He held up an empty box.

"Just this," he said, the corners of his mouth upturned into a knowing sneer, his eyes sparkled.

"Wow." Scottie took the evidence bag, spinning it over several times to get a better look and handed it back. "Anything else?"

"Nothing."

"No porn, eh?" Scottie joked.

"Was that a question or a remark?" Gibson asked stiffly, not one to tolerate any mockery.

Scottie was a little flustered, "Didn't mean to suggest it like that. Maybe just an inkling about Robbie." Scottie hesitated. "You know his orientation."

"Yeah. I suppose you're right," Gibson admitted. He patted Scottie's shoulder lightly. "But nothing there."

"Should we check the other building?"

"Definitely."

They crossed the courtyard. Gibson turned at the door and saw Jason move away from the second-floor window. The workshop was an immense space with long workbenches on opposite sides. Tools and parts littered the countertops. Bulky jackets and pants were hung chaotically on hooks along the back wall. Tony's office was tucked in the far corner. A cursory look into the washroom next to it revealed another dirty scene. Gibson puckered his mouth in disgust.

"Time for a coffee."

"Good idea."

As they moved down the street, a vehicle crept into the maintenance yard. Andrew sat in his vehicle for a moment. The stillness was creepy—a murder had happened there this morning. What the hell was he doing here? He headed home, forgetting about his appointment at three.

The foreman remained behind the blinds squinting at the visitor. What does he want? The Mustang pulled out. Jason went back to his desk.

Chapter 11

On the northeast side of the campus was a trendy café called the Ottiva. AJ had given Scottie a heads up on its popularity with the university crowd. The coffee was exceptional and the home-cooked food comforting. But its popularity meant it was jam-packed all day. Scottie pulled into a spot close to the restaurant, and they strode quickly down the sidewalk to avoid getting drowned by the rain now coming down in buckets. As soon as she swung the door open, they could smell the sweet aroma of freshly baked pastry and savoury spices. They found an unoccupied space by the entrance and sat down on the wooden chairs. The table wobbled when Gibson placed his elbow on top. Each time another customer arrived or left, they got a blast of bracing sea air. Despite the commotion, the fresh steaming cups of coffee made it all worthwhile. It was a pleasant atmosphere, unpretentious and friendly. They remained silent, each mulling over the day's developments. After several minutes of congenial contemplation Scottie spoke up.

"So, what do you think?"

"I know every workplace has its token bully, but this place is loaded with them," Gibson said. Then he put his journal on the table and opened it to the first page. He thumbed through his observations and looked up at her. "Tim is the most obvious bully and Nick is his sidekick." He paused and added, "Nick's hiding something."

"What about David?"

"He's a loner. I'm certain he knows more about what's going on here." Gibson stopped to consider. "Maybe he's afraid to say something."

"Afraid of what?" Scottie gave him an incredulous eye.

"I don't know. Getting beaten up. Or worse."

"By whom. Tim?"

"Probably. Maybe." He shrugged. He tried not to dislike the individuals he met while working a murder crime. It clouded his impartiality. But he had Tim in his sights. He hated bullies more than anything. They pressured weaker people to do their bidding. It was an outrage that boiled his blood.

"Jason is a cocky guy," Scottie said.

"Isn't he? But he also wants to be everybody's friend. He rides with the crew at the bike park."

"Oh, yeah. And the other boss too. What a piece of work. He has a malicious streak."

Gibson nodded in compliance. "Is this a hate crime?"

"I'm not sure. The condom was planted so…" She lost her thought.

"Someone wanted us to know that Robbie was gay." Gibson picked up the trail.

"Maybe."

"We can't ignore the bully factor. And if Robbie was gay…"

Gibson knew Scottie had a conflicting view from him and wasn't ready to call this a hate crime. He could tell by how she squirmed in her chair. He couldn't figure out why she hesitated because she had felt the effects of that kind of thinking herself—people judging her because she was a lesbian.

"We still have to visit Robbie's wife and break the news," Gibson said. "I've asked the others to leave that to us."

"Okay." A slight wavering of her voice was evident.

That was another thing Gibson knew about Scottie. She hated this part of the job. It was always awkward and heartbreaking especially when kids were involved. It affected him too. Although Scottie didn't have kids of her own, she was devoted to her nieces. If something happened to her sister there would be nothing left but a void, a swirling blackness. He prayed that would never happen. The coffee had renewed their energy. They were as prepared as they could be to break the news to Ellen. Outside the sun gleamed for brief moments, clouds quickly racing in to fill the blue patches.

"What's the house number?" Gibson asked as they approached Henderson Road.

Scottie took out her notebook from a top pocket and tossed it over. At the front of the pad were the contacts compiled from the interviews. Gibson ran his finger down the list and found Robbie and Ellen Spencer.

"107."

Children were playing outside on the lawn as they pulled up to the curb. More kids and a dog rushed around the corner of the house. The long-haired beast bounced wildly from person to person. Laughter echoed throughout the neighbourhood. They walked down the pavement past all the pandemonium and up the stairs to the veranda. Trying to force back their sombre mood, they stopped for a moment to brace themselves. Mayhem usually followed lousy news. Scottie rang the doorbell and then stepped aside. The door was open by a six-year-old girl with curly blonde hair and bright eyes. She remained motionless in her pink frock and lacy socks pulled up tight.

"Hello there," Gibson said. "Is your mom home?"

"Mm-huh," the little girl said timidly, swaying back and forth on her tippy-toes.

"Lily. Who is it?" A shout came from the rear.

The little girl continued to dance on her toes. Her mother approached from the hallway and halted when she saw them. Neither Gibson nor Scottie wore uniforms, but their suits and haircuts gave away their identity.

"Has something happened?" Ellen stepped forward, her body stiffening. She had short-cropped red hair that ended bluntly at the nape. Her youthful complexion was rosy and makeup free. She stood stoically waiting to hear what tragedy had befallen her family. Her skin paled and the lines around her eyes deepened.

"May we come in?"

"This way."

They accompanied her down the cramped hallway, dodging the abandoned toys and boxes. The dim lighting and bare walls gave the appearance of neglect. But then they reached a doorway that opened into a bright and cheery kitchen filled with the delicious smell of cookies and hot chocolate. The girl had followed them into this inviting area.

"Go watch a little TV, Lily. Then we'll have treats," Ellen urged. "Okay?" It almost turned into a plea as her voice rose two octaves. She smiled warmly after Lily as she left the room.

"Robbie is dead. We're sorry for your loss," Gibson said. There was no easy way.

Ellen let out the smallest of sobs and crumpled into a chair. Outside they could pick up the glees of children playing and the dog yapping. Inside, Ellen had gone quiet. Her entire face seemed drained, aging ten years as the moments ticked along.

"He was murdered."

"Murdered? Why?"

"Did Robbie have any enemies at work? Anyone who would want to harm him?"

"No." Her facial muscles were slack and her eyes had stopped blinking.

Gibson wasn't sure if she felt everything or nothing.

Lily had come back into the room and settled her head on her mother's lap. Ellen stroked her soft baby curls tenderly and spoke softly. Gibson thought she was singing a lullaby. She looked up at him with mournful eyes.

"The guys are always picking on him. About his biking and his shorts…" she said. "Was it one of them?"

"We don't know."

"What will I do?" She breathed in deeply.

"Is there someone we can call?"

"No. We'll be okay. I need to be alone now." She pushed a lock of hair from Lily's face.

"We'll see ourselves out," Gibson said.

The detectives walked down the hallway. A short sob followed them out and then stopped almost at once. They stepped outside to the children still playing on the front lawn, rolling over each other like steam shovels and falling apart with laughter.

Chapter 12

The rain stopped late that afternoon. Heavy clouds had broken up, leaving behind a few lonely sentinels above. The sun, angled low in the autumn sky, shone pale against the dark blue backdrop. Gibson breathed a sigh of relief when he rounded the final corner to his house. A beacon set up high on a pole gleamed brightly at the end of the driveway. He had installed it when they had first moved here. The light had transformed the sombre, narrow lane into a safe, inviting road. He pulled into the drive and killed the engine. The glow of the lights that streamed from within the home beckoned him in. He got out of his F150 and paused, taking in the loveliness of the neighbourhood. He could hear the peaceful lapping of waves on the shoreline below, the twittering of birds as they dashed from tree to tree and an occasional slam of a door in the distance. A barely perceptible current of air from the Southeast crept up the bank and touched his cheek.

"Hi, Katherine," Gibson called out as he stepped through the door. Spicy aromas wafted from the back. She appeared in the kitchen entrance with a flour-dusted apron hung from her waist and spoon clutched in hand.

"You're just in time."

"Whatever it is, smells fantastic," he said as he removed his boots and coat. He gave her a tender hug and caressed her ear with his cool lips.

"It is fantastic."

"Can I help with anything?" It was really a rhetorical question.

"Go wash up and I'll serve gourmet delights," she said with a grin, turning back to the kitchen.

After dinner Katherine cleared the table. Then she busied herself arranging appetizers on china platters and uncorking several bottles of Okanagan red wine for the evening's company. Gibson got a fire started in the airtight. Before long it blazed brightly, heating the living room and spilling the warmth throughout the house. He helped himself to a beer and sat back to unwind after a harrowing day. Their guests were expected within the hour. The finches chirped happily in the corner. A sharp tap on the door stirred Gibson from his nap. He hauled himself off the couch and answered the summons.

"Welcome."

Andrew and Heather stood on the stoop, arm in arm, and all smiles.

"Hello," Heather said. She hugged him and headed for the kitchen.

"Hi there," Andrew shouted down the hallway to Katherine. He gave Gibson a hardy handshake.

"Make yourself at home. Gibson will get you a drink," Katherine yelled back.

"Like she had to tell me that."

They glanced at each other and chuckled. Andrew settled into the cushions of the cozy sofa. Immediately his attention was drawn to the fireplace, the golden flames flickering wildly behind glass doors. His eyelids drooped as the mesmerizing fire danced, sending out waves of warmth.

"Yeah. I fell asleep right there," Gibson said. He was seated in a chair farthest from the heat. A precaution for staying awake.

Soon they were all hunkered down and comfortably immersed in conversation, sipping their drinks and sampling the finger food. This evening Katherine had her hair pinned up with rhinestone clips. A deep shade of metallic bronze eye shadow highlighted the brown cascades of curls bouncing off her shoulders. She wore casual jeans and a rich cocoa coloured sweater, looking serene and snug sunk into the over-stuffed loveseat with her friend leaning into her.

"Andrew was telling us about his blog today," Katherine said.

"That's right," Andrew confirmed. "Sex and death."

"We got sidetracked," Heather spoke up. "Tell us more."

"She means gossipy details." Katherine struggled to keep a straight face but failed. Heather stuck her tongue out.

"Read the blog." Andrew chuckled.

Katherine punched his arm. Heather flashed her saucy smile.

"Any details you can share about what happened today?" Heather asked.

"We just got started so there are lots of leads we have to follow." Gibson hedged, not wanting to share his thoughts.

"Who was murdered?" Andrew blurted out and promptly bit his lip. Damn.

"It was Robbie Spencer. Medium height, sandy blonde hair. Works for maintenance. Do you know him?"

"No. I don't think so," Andrew said, letting out a big sigh of relief.

"This is getting too morbid. Let's go for a walk." Katherine stood up and stretched. She tugged on Heather's hand to get her moving. "It's stifling in here."

She was greeted with groans all round. But gradually, they bundled up to enjoy a stroll along the waterway. The moon was high in the sky, lighting up the route, the trees and the distant snow-capped mountains.

Gibson wondered about his brother-in-law. Was something going on?

* * *

David spent the rest of the day in his garage toying with his tired blue Jeep. He had just added the final coat of polish on the faded yellow and orange sun depicted on the hood. His wife had confiscated the garage for her car, so he was allocated to the driveway where the sunlight had beat the hell out of the paint job. He heard a vehicle stop at the curb. The door squeaked opened and then slammed shut. David looked up fearing the worst. The handlebars peeking out from the cargo bed were from a Specialized mountain bike, orange with white stripes, brand-new. Shit. Tim came around the rear of the truck dressed in his riding outfit, long sleeve jersey shirt and pants. On top of this, he had a full storm trooper set of body armour with shin, knee and elbow pads for protection and a baseball cap. He swung his LED bike light by his side.

"Hey. Ready to ride in the dark?" Tim asked, kicking his foot in the gravel in the annoying way he always did. "Jason and Nick are coming."

"Don't think so." He wasn't up to listening to all their bullshit. Not after today's events. He continued rubbing at the polish, ignoring Tim.

"Why not? What's the problem?"

"Busy." David kept his eyes averted knowing Tim had a lot more to spout.

"What were you telling that detective?" He moved in closer to his prey.

"Nothing."

"You better not mention anything about the fight," he warned and narrowed his eyes. "Or did you already spill the beans? I think you did."

"What! That the 'golden boy' is a troublemaker," David countered and then added, "capable of who knows what."

Tim stepped in tight to David and glanced over his shoulder. Probably to make sure no one was watching his antics.

"Better not say anything. Don't make this personal." His lips quivered, hands fisted at his side.

David bumped into the bucket as he fumbled backward. It tipped onto the drive and spilled the last of the soapy water.

"Look what you did." He stepped forward. "The truth will get out no matter what I do or do not say." The snarl on his lips tempted Tim to make a foolish move, but he abstained and twisted away.

"You, asshole."

Tim jumped in his truck and spun out his tires.

David turned to see Jackie standing at the top of the stairs. Her cotton top hung loosely over her slender frame. She had that Mediterranean appearance with her aquiline nose, almond-shaped eyes and olive-bronzed skin. Her Scandinavian straw-like blonde hair was twisted into a bun. The mixture of cultures made it easy to look at her.

"What a jerk."

"Frigging ass," he growled. His body vibrated uncontrollably from the confrontation.

"What else can you say?"

"Nothing," David conceded as he cooled down. He picked up his rag and continued buffing the hood, more resolutely than before.

Chapter 13

Gibson was sitting behind his desk at VIIMCU, the major crime unit. The inconspicuous building was located on Dallas Road in a row of commercial type structures. From his million-dollar view, the open ocean stretched before him. The sailboats below were mere drops of colour. In the distance, the majestic Olympic Mountains seemed to soar out of the strait. Snow on their caps stayed all year round with sunlight glinting off the whiteness.

The three-storey low rise was made of concrete and mirrored glass. Thousands of panes cast back the diversity of the street and the sun's golden rays. The front entrance had no signage to reveal its government designation. Big glass doors opened into a spacious lobby. A modest cafeteria for the force was tucked in the corner of the building on the first floor. Few civilians were allowed so the seats were filled with employees. The rest of the floor held the Forensic Identification section where the crime scene unit processed fingerprints, DNA, hair, fibres and photographic evidence. The third floor contained the newly set up Bomb Squad. A specially trained Vancouver team used to take the ferry over if the situation called for defusing an explosive. It had been a waiting game that took up to nine hours to get the job done. Now Victoria had its own unit to handle detonations. It made sense and was a relief to police officials.

The second floor was Gibson's realm. It was partitioned into several rooms at the front, and a huge boardroom and interview chambers at the back. His office was a small elegant room with soft carpeting, blue-grey surfaces and lots of light streaming in from the many windows. There were prints in silver frames hung on one wall. His desk faced the corner window and was efficiently organized with stand-up filing racks and a laptop. Beside it were an extensive filing cabinet and a bookcase. At the door there was an old-fashioned hat and coat rack that he had discovered during an expedition down Fort Street on Antique Row. He had several men that served under his guidance. Scottie and three detective constables had their offices across from him.

His supervisor, Police Chief Rex Shafer, worked out of the central station on Caledonia Street. Rex rarely interfered with the operations at the major crime unit but always kept his finger in the pie. He would give opinions, ask questions and wanted to be informed of any progress. Requests for assistance from other districts came in occasionally, and Rex had no compunction about sending someone from the task force to go.

Gibson sunk into the softness and sweet smell of his leather armchair and inhaled its richness. Just as he picked up his cell to make a call, the landline buzzed.

"Gibson."

"What have you got so far?" It was the police chief. "I heard something I don't want to hear."

"Okay." His boss was all political so he knew what was coming next.

"Don't turn this into a hate crime. We don't need that. Understood?" Rex asked gruffly. "Follow the money. That's my motto," he added with confidence.

"Yes, Chief," Gibson conceded. He always complied. Then he let the investigation take him where it led.

"Okay. Keep me posted," Rex said, pacified for the moment. "You have Gunner on the case?"

"Yes."

"Good. Good," the chief said and hung up.

Gunner was the one trouble spot in his department. He was the chief's nephew, his sister's boy. Lots of tomfoolery but untouchable. Gibson stood up and wandered over to the window. Looking down onto the road, traffic was sparse as it commonly was here. Most vehicles were headed to the cruise ships docked at the quay or the helicopter terminal next to it. A few bicycles zoomed past, en route to Beacon Park trails at the top of the road. On weekends there was a continuous flow of riders. The phone ringing jarred him from faraway thoughts of mountains, of ocean water, of peaceful moments in his kayak.

"Gibson."

"Hi. I can give you the highlights of the autopsy," Rod said. "Only one surprise."

"What's that?" He leaned against the desktop and crossed his legs to get comfortable. The ME could be long-winded.

"First, the strike on his cranium caused death," Rod said. "It appears he was kneeling down when he was attacked." Neither man spoke. Gibson could hear buzzing coming down the phone line. He remained quiet, curious to see where this was leading. Finally Rod went on, "He could have just been tying his shoelace. I'll leave that to you."

Gibson grunted.

"Second. No drugs or alcohol. Third, it took place between five-thirty and seven in the morning. I could tighten the time a little. Maybe."

"And last." Rod paused before he proceeded, making sure he had Gibson's complete attention. "There wasn't any suggestion of sexual activity. Considering there was a condom at the scene…" He let the sentence linger.

"Tell me about the condom. What does it signify?"

"It's at the lab. Talk to Jocko. What's his last name again?"

"I don't think I ever knew it. It's always been just Jocko."

"Okay, sure. Anyways, I'll shoot the autopsy report over later this morning. The rest is your job: to figure out why."

Rod hung up before he could comment.

He heard a commotion in the corridor, a thundering sound and whooping. Two constables halted in the doorway.

"I vote for the homeless guy," Gunner said.

"Gentlemen, please have a seat," Gibson said, designating the chairs in front of his desk. "I hope you aren't joking about this case." He stared critically at Gunner, a cold glint in his steel-grey eyes. Na grew quiet.

"We met the homeless guy, and I tell you—" He stopped after a jab into his ribs by Na. Gunner looked up at his boss. He tried to see into the depth of Gibson's gaze but failed. His chin dropped to his chest. "Sorry."

Gibson controlled his annoyance at the impertinence of the constable and said coolly, "I expect more from you. Some regard for people's differences and rights." Although he recognized Na wasn't implicated in the mocking, he hadn't thwarted it either. He peered at Na and said, "You should know better. Am I clear, gentlemen?"

"Yes, sir," both men responded and sat up straighter. Gunner wiped the smirk off his face. Na looked serious with his mouth pulled down into a frown.

"Did you find anything in the parking lot?" Gibson asked after a lengthy silence.

"No, sir, nothing there," Na said. Gunner agreed.

"Give me the low-down on the homeless encampment."

"We headed over to that spot by the edge of the park. The clearing where they hang out overnight. We hoped to get there before everyone split," Gunner said.

"Good plan. What did you find?"

"There was only one guy there. Said he didn't know anything but started to rant about always getting hassled."

"By whom."

"I expect he meant the workers, because he flapped his hands over to the maintenance yard. He said he sees this guy riding his bike all the time from there."

"So you assume he was referring to Robbie?"

"Yeah. So we asked him if he saw the biker this morning. But he said no."

"Anything else I need to know?"

"We checked out his pack to see if he had Robbie's wallet. He really put up a fuss about that. Saying stuff like we're tampering with his personal property and constitutional rights."

Gibson raised his eyebrows.

"Scottie told us it was missing before she dispatched us."

"Okay. Did you find anything?"

"He had a lot of cash which was peculiar in itself but no wallet," Gunner said. "So we left him and knocked on more doors."

"Go on."

"We found a neighbour that lives right next to the maintenance building. He saw a homeless guy hanging around."

Gibson looked up with interest.

"We questioned him further, and he backed off. Said they all hang out at the garbage bins. It sounded like the gentleman was just complaining. I don't think he saw anything in particular yesterday morning."

"Okay. We'll get back to him if we need to. The camp probably isn't involved. What would the motive be?" He paused. "Anything else?"

"Yeah. A man on the other side of the park was walking his dog early yesterday morning," Na said. He checked his notes before adding, "Around six o'clock. He saw a truck parked on the main boulevard. It had writing on the door, but he couldn't read what it said. He didn't have his glasses on. And he wasn't sure if anyone was in the truck. Anyways it didn't seem suspicious to him."

Gunner barged in, "Too vague to be any help right now, but we have him in our report in case he remembers anything solid."

"Keep looking. Something will show up when you least expect it."

"You bet. We'll canvass the area again. Not everyone was up yet," Gunner said.

Gibson was slumped in his chair already thinking of other stuff—Robbie's spouse. One of the worst things about the job was questioning the victim's partner. Not usual for the wife to kill her husband. But it happens. Gunner and Na sensed this was the end of the conversation. Gibson was rubbing his face and staring off at nothing. They pushed their chairs away from the desk and quietly left the room.

* * *

AJ had arrived extra early for work because yesterday had been cut short with all the excitement. Turmoil expressed it better. He had an extensive project to finish by the end of the week. After an hour of hammering on metal plates, he got a craving for nicotine. The clock hanging by Tony's office chimed six. Still time before the guys would roll in. He grabbed his pack of poison and slipped out the back for a brief puff. He sucked in the smoke deeply, inclined his face skyward and streamed out broad, perfect circles. After a few minutes, a shiver shot up his spine from a brisk breeze whipping around the corner. He tossed his butt on the ground, crushed it with the toe of his work boots and swung the door open to get back to work, to the warmth.

A whack on his head sent him sprawling with a face plant to the cement floor. His eyesight blurred and everything went black. He awoke with a ringing in his ears and someone tugging on his shirt sleeve.

"Are you okay?"

It hurt to open his eyes. The dim overhead lights shone as if someone was directing a spotlight on his face. He raised his chin slightly and felt his brain reel. Stars drifted into his vision.

"AJ," Keith said.

He attempted another look—the stars had retired. His brain stopped spinning.

"I'm fine." He patted the back of his hair and fingered a tacky substance.

The assistant supervisor helped him to his feet.

"What happened?"

"I don't know. Somebody thumped me when I came back into the shop."

"You're bleeding."

"It's nothing. Forget it. I'm good." AJ shrugged him off and escaped to the restroom. A gash on his forehead leaked blood down his cheek. He bandaged the laceration on his face, but there was nothing he could do about the bump on his head except pop a few aspirin.

Keith was hovering near the door, but AJ pushed his way by and headed to his workbench. He beat on the metal feverishly in spite of his pounding head, wondering who had done this to him. He twisted his mouth into a scowl and turned his narrowed eyes toward Keith—get out and shut up.

Chapter 14

Gibson went back to the window to shake the foreboding thoughts from his mind. His preoccupation with husbands and wives brought Katherine to mind. Was she busy in her greenhouse today? Or sitting on the bed crying for things past? Slowly he focused on an enormous cruise ship docking, perhaps returning from an Alaskan trip. He watched as taxi after taxi drove into the terminal to stand by in a lengthy line of vehicles. Suddenly Gibson realized the breeze had dropped to a peculiar stillness. Sailboats that had been flirting with the wind and waves now puttered to the harbour with their mainsails and jibs furled. A soft tap on the door caught his attention, and he turned towards it.

"Hi, Billy." Scottie stepped into the room and approached him.

"Should we go see Ellen this morning?"

"Yeah, I guess."

Gibson grabbed his jacket, and they made their way down the stairs, past the unoccupied receptionist desk and out the front door. They hopped into Scottie's truck and headed to the suburbs. The vehicle hummed through the side streets. He stared out the window and let his eyes stray over the landscape. The trees were silhouetted against the pastel blue sky. Under the naked branches, shed leaves made a pulpy mass. A few juncos scratched through the grass for gnats and bugs. Nuthatches and chickadees flitted from one tree to the next, always on the move. A squirrel ran in front of the vehicle. Scottie avoided the little guy with her superb reflexes, barely blinking an eye. She rambled on about Ellen and Robbie's marriage. How did the condom play into their relationship? Was he cheating on her? Gibson saw the sideways glance she risked to determine if he was taking notice. He grunted in reply so she went on chatting about the kids and the effect this would have on them.

"They're too young to understand that," Gibson said.

"I'm not sure I follow you."

"The condom," he replied and gazed momentarily at Scottie. Her Roman nose in profile emphasized the prominent high bridge and looked remarkably like the curved beak of an eagle—a sign of beauty and nobility.

"Oh, I meant his death."

Gibson picked up on her meaning and became silent again. She turned down Henderson Road, pulled up to the curb and shut off the motor. They exited the truck and strode down the pathway to the wooden veranda. No children were playing on the grass. Gibson hadn't noticed much when they visited yesterday. Now he saw that the house had a fresh coat of paint, a creamy shade of white. The porch was a darker grey than the trim. As he climbed the steps, he saw peeling paint under his boots. He wondered who would complete the work. Lily opened the door in response to the bell. She twirled down the hallway, leaving them waiting helplessly on the veranda. He could hear a muffled drone of a television in the direction the little girl had retreated. No sweet smells of baking this time, just an uncanny hollowness.

Ellen came out of the living room, dragging her chewed up pink slippers along the carpet. She was dressed in sweatpants, her hair hanging limply in greasy strands. Her face was puffy and drawn with a jaw clenched tight. She showed them into the room. Two large couches dominated the area with a fireplace on the far side. She perched on the sofa closest to it. Was she expecting to feel warmth from the unlit fire? Gibson wondered. The giant pillows swallowed her fidgeting body. He chose an armchair that faced her. Scottie lingered in the background, standing with a notebook and pen ready.

"We have a few questions for you today," Gibson said. "Can you tell me about the party? Did the whole family go?"

"Party?" Ellen fluttered her eyelids as she looked up at him.

"The Halloween celebration," Gibson reminded her.

"The kids came with us. But I took them home early. Robbie stayed."

"When did he get in?" Before she could respond, he added, "And when did he leave for work?"

"He got in around midnight. I think he left at his regular time. Sometime after six." She twisted a damp handkerchief in her hands.

A truck rumbled by and shook the windows in its wake. Gibson looked out to the street. Ellen had gone quiet.

"Is there any other family besides his half-brother?"

Ellen raised her chin, her face streaked with a mixture of mascara and emotion. "Oh no. Jeff. I forgot. He doesn't know yet." A frown appeared as she pulled on the arms of her chair.

"Don't worry. We'll talk to him." Gibson sprung out of his chair to stop her motion.

"There's no one else. Just me and the kids." As she spoke, a torrent of tears drenched her cheeks.

He stole a glance toward Scottie. They left Ellen to her emptiness.

Chapter 15

Foul Bay Road was just around the corner. Scottie pulled to the curb and parked. They walked up the cracked sidewalk to Jeff's house. The garish green and yellow gables, powder blue handrails and turquoise trim were typical décors for this gentrified neighbourhood. Scottie knocked, paused and waited for an answer. She knocked again. Gibson noticed there weren't any vehicles around. He tapped her forearm and gestured to the driveway.

"I don't think anybody's home."

Then the door swung open. As skinny as Robbie had been, his half-brother Jeff was substantially bulkier. His pants hung loosely below the waistline. Matted brown hair was plastered to his forehead and a whisper of a tattoo peeked from under his tee-shirt at the shoulder. Was that a flying pig? Scottie towered over him by almost a foot. The contrast in their heights emphasized the man's stocky build.

"Jeff Stewart?" Scottie questioned, a little gruffly.

"Yes. What do you want?" Jeff asked with exasperated impatience.

"It's about Robbie," Scottie said, toning it down. "May we come in?"

"What about him? I'm kind of busy."

"He's dead," Gibson butt in.

"What?"

"Murdered."

"That's bullshit." Jeff stepped back. His mouth opened and closed like he was gasping for breath. The sickly smell of instant sweat assailed their nostrils. His eyes flickered, and he turned into the house. Without an invitation, they followed him down a narrow hallway to a miserable living room. The mixture of stale cigarettes and musty air stopped their breath short. The lighting was mute and made dimmer by the smoky atmosphere. Only a single ray of sunlight found its way past the drab curtains, possibly drawn closed to block out prying eyes. The stark furnishings called attention to the dinginess of the space. There was an overstuffed couch with frayed armrests and burn holes in the cushions. A tattered blanket was draped down to the floor—doubtless where Jeff had been napping. Rickety second-hand chairs and a coffee table covered with greasy plates and overflowing ashtrays completed the scene. The drape jammed on its warped wooden pole as Jeff pushed on it with some difficulty. Finally a glimmer of light forced its way through the dirt-laden windows.

Jeff waved them to sit. Walking across the carpet sent clouds of dust flying. Scottie clamped her mouth tight and pulled her palm over her nose, barely inhaling—fearful of foreign debris floating into her lungs. Jeff flung himself back onto the couch, snatching a cigarette and drumming it on his thigh. The detectives sat squatted on the edge of their chairs, hoping not to stain their clothes or worst—find bugs crawling up their pant legs. Scottie opened her notebook and produced a pen from an inside jacket pocket.

Gibson started by saying he was sorry for his loss. He rapped off the traditional rhetoric begrudgingly. There was an unpleasant quality about Jeff.

"We didn't get along particularly well," Jeff snorted.

The detectives remained silent. Not only to stop themselves from saying something regrettable but to see if Jeff would continue talking. Bingo!

"But it's shocking. We talked sometimes. What happened anyway?" Jeff flogged his cigarette on his leg more forcibly.

Gibson gave him a lowdown of the crime leaving out details that only the killer would know. Jeff pulled away from the onslaught of ghastly facts, his ruddy complexion paling quickly. His feet jiggled on the worn-out rug. He plucked up a lighter off the coffee table, and then tossed it back without any thought.

"Do you play baseball, Jeff?" Gibson asked. The tone of his voice revealed his dislike of the brother—half-brother.

"Sure."

"Robbie was struck with a bat."

"It wasn't mine!" The pitch in his voice had gone from bass to alto.

"Were you at the party with Robbie?"

"Yeah," Jeff answered, uncertain how one question had led to another.

"So you hung out occasionally as well it seems," Gibson said. "Tell me."

Jeff leaned forward, twirling the cigarette in his fingers. The slightest curve at the corner of his mouth appeared, a coldness crept into his eyes.

"Ellen invited me. She's always trying to get us to mend bridges." He paused and peered at them. A smirk playing on his face showed yellowed teeth. "So I showed up at the party in my Sunday best. Cause you never know. I hooked up with this nice young woman." He showed a voluptuous shape with his hands, gave a wink and settled back in his chair with an exaggerated casualness.

Gibson set his steel-grey eyes into a stony stare.

"What's her name?" he barked.

"I don't know. The lady was in a costume," Jeff said. "But then she split all of a sudden. I don't know why. Anyway, I went home." The grin had vanished. He tossed the unlit cigarette onto the table and played with the silver earring hanging from his pierced ear.

"And the next morning?"

"I was here. Sleeping. The girl split like I said." He dropped his gaze, rubbing his forehead to mask his chagrin.

Just then Gibson's phone buzzed.

"Gibson." He escaped from the stifling room and stood in the hallway.

"Jocko. Here at the lab."

Gibson closed his eyes and waited for the news.

"The blood on the bat is from Robbie Spencer. I got a good set of prints from the handle. There was also a sticker on it with initials. JS." Gibson heard him shuffle paper. "Oh yeah. Nothing interesting with the backpack. Only Robbie's blood."

"The condom wrapping?"

"No prints."

"What. Isn't that kind of weird?" Gibson groaned.

"Somebody wiped it."

"Oh, really." He thanked Jocko, hung up and stepped back into the gloomy room. He looked at Scottie and said, "Get his prints?"

"What? You can't do that," Jeff protested.

"I think the bat is yours. There's a label on it with your initials. So yeah, we have good reason to take your prints."

"It's not mine."

But they got his prints nevertheless. Now with some physical evidence, they went hunting for prints from everybody possible.

* * *

Katherine was in the greenhouse with Heather, steaming mugs of chamomile tea warming their palms.

Wispy bangs tickled the side of Heather's left cheek. She leaned forward with interest as Katherine spoke, unfolding her legs and adjusting the folds of her red dress.

"Chamomile is an excellent herb for combating anxiety and depression," Katherine said. She had spent a sleepless night tossing and turning—many sleepless nights. She was trying to get the business diploma she had deserted a long time ago. As the exam date got closer, the knot in her gut got bigger.

"You know a lot about herbs," Heather said. "I love cooking and should use them more."

Katherine sensed that her friend wanted to draw the conversation away from her despondent spirits. But she was in a melancholy mood and could not be swayed to alter her gloomy state of mind.

"I've been thinking about my ex." A crease was forming between her eyebrows as she talked. She rubbed at it to release the tension, but it wouldn't go away.

"Oh, Katherine," Heather exclaimed. She had been strumming her nails on the side of her mug. This remark caused her to stop midway to the next tap and look intently at her friend.

Katherine waved a hand backward to ward off the sympathy. She rubbed at her forehead again, trying to erase the subsequent thought.

"And my miscarriage. It was awful."

A blush fluttered up Heather's face. She pressed her lips together and picked at her nail polish nervously. Katherine ignored her friend's weird reaction and carried on with her story.

"Just living with Arthur and his bullying started my panic attacks. Then the…" she floundered, stopping her thoughts midflight. Her mouth went dry. She felt a shiver run up her back and a clammy sheen break out on her cheeks. But she was beyond crying at this point so she squeezed her eyes shut and blurted out the ending.

"I lost the baby."

Heather reached over and stroked her friend's trembling hands with tender caresses. Her touch was warm against the dampness of her friend's skin. Before Katherine could speak, she raised a finger to her mouth and shook her head. There were no words for this moment. Heather remained still as her friend fidgeted on her stool. Katherine scrunched up her face and then released the tension, struggling to regain composure. As her apprehension eased, the wrinkles that had appeared around her lips smoothed. She gave Heather a timid grin, breathed in deeply and pulled her hands away.

"I'm okay. Let's talk about the gourmet cook."

"Yes, this gourmet cook needs lessons on infusing herbs into her creations." Heather blew out a giant exhalation of pent-up breath and took a sip of her cold tea.

Katherine glanced up at the clock with its whimsical numbers daring her to decipher the correct time. An hour had slipped by. They had been delving into a variety of aromatic plants to use with beef, lamb or chicken. Rubbing the leaves of each different spice released a plethora of fragrance in the greenhouse.

"How are your classes coming along?" Heather dared to ask.

"Considering all, it's going smoothly. The final is coming up fast though." Another shudder shot up her spine.

"Cool."

"You're right. It is cool." Katherine hesitated. "Imagine me getting a diploma." She failed to stop herself from smiling.

Heather lifted an eyebrow and pinched her friend's arm playfully.

"That's better. It's a dream come true!"

* * *

Jeff lived close to the university so it took the detectives only a few moments to get to the maintenance buildings. Scottie parked on the street. They stepped out of the vehicle and braced against the gale that had sprung up. The blustery Northeast gusts propelled dirt into their eyes. With their heads carried low, they approached the garage. Even with the howling, they could hear an acrimonious dispute emanating from within. Gibson walked over, stopping shy of the door. A lull in the wind allowed the crushing of gravel under his feet to become perceptible. Jason stopped yelling. He swung toward the intruder, leaned against the Zamboni and smiled contemptuously. David stood with his hands by his side and rocked in his boots, trying to dodge the rant.

Tim exchanged a look with Gibson and beamed with satisfaction. He was obviously revelling in the aggressive onslaught directed at someone else. Disgusted, Gibson turned on an axis, grabbing Scottie's arm as he reversed directions. They cut across the courtyard in a few strides and opened the shop door in pursuit of the supervisor. Tony was sitting on a stool, swivelling back and forth mindlessly, evidently accomplishing nothing. The crew was hanging about, perched on stools or leaned against the rear counter. AJ stood in front of a bench with a welded bracket. He was smoothing the rough edges and talking to a worker between strokes of the file. Shouldn't they be out there working, Gibson thought. Or maybe it was an extended coffee break?

"What now?" Tony asked in an exceedingly unpleasant tone. "Can't you see I'm busy?"

"We would like to take everybody's fingerprints," Gibson said. "All present. Makes my job simpler."

"What for?" Tony demanded.

"Just for elimination. Any objections?"

Nobody objected but Tony ranted anyways.

"As I previously explained we were in a safety meeting." Tony made an ugly grin. "Did you find out whose bat it was?" he asked, curiosity kicking in. He stared at the detectives. Gibson ignored him.

Scottie had arranged a fingerprinting kit on a worktable. After printing each man's name on a separate card, she signalled to one of the crew. AJ strolled over and held his palms up as if in submission. The gang laughed at his shenanigans. She picked up AJ's hand and rolled his finger in the ink to cover the entire tip. Then each finger was pushed onto the prepared card. After the procedure she gave him a moisture package to wash off the residue and a pen to sign the label. She moved through the list of names, stamping each person's prints with care. When Scottie was finished, she deposited the completed sheets into evidence bags and planted them in the case. Gibson strolled over to the bench closest to Tony and leaned against it with his hip, setting his hand against the coarse surface.

"So no one quit the meeting early?" A shuffling of feet caught his attention. He glanced up to see AJ with an idiotic grin on his face look down at his project.

"No, and I resent all the insinuation," Tony said.

"What about the guys in the other shop? Do you want to alibi them as well?" Gibson asked. He was trying to control his annoyance.

"I expect you're barking up the wrong tree. Everyone gets along in Jason's department," Tony said. "He has loads of experience running a tight crew. All the guys like him."

"So, no conflict," Gibson sneered. "Oh yeah, except there was that fight between Robbie and Tim." He was determined to find out what had gone on.

"Just a little fisticuffs. Boys will be boys." Tony shifted his position on his stool.

Gibson saw him throw a sly glance toward AJ. Was that a warning? What was up with the Band-Aid on AJ's face? Did he get into a scuffle too? Tony turned back and presented his most honest face, holding back the sneer at the corner of his mouth. Not only had Gibson witnessed tension between Jason and the crew, but Tony's attitude and body language defied his remarks. He stood up and folded his arms over his chest. Suspicion about Tony lingered. What was Tony hiding? Was it a part of this investigation? Or something else? He looked across the room at Scottie. The sergeant was standing with one hand on her hip and the other clutching the fingerprint case. They took off. Na and Gunner were leaning against the building when they stepped into the courtyard.

"What's up?"

"We saw Scottie's vehicle on the street," Na said. "Figured we'd touch base."

Gibson waited.

"We haven't gotten any further so we're headed to the office. We have statements to prepare. Gunner wants to check social media, too." Na swung away with his partner following close behind.

"What social media?"

Na stopped abruptly. Gunner was looking at his feet and bumped into him.

"Sorry." Gunner collected himself. "Facebook. It's amazing what people will post."

"Excellent idea. Could you guys hang out for a bit? I just need to get a few more prints. Would you be able to drop them off to Jocko?"

"Sure. We'll wait in the car if that's okay," Na said. A burst of cold air rattled the garage doors as he spoke.

"Much appreciated." Gibson chuckled and motioned with a toss of his hand.

The tape from the crime scene was gone so they used the main entrance to get in the building. The stain on the wall hadn't washed out entirely. A faint trail of blood still showed through. Gibson pulled up his sleeve and looked at his watch. Past one. He hoped these guys had an extended lunch hour too. He opened the door to the garage, but nobody was there so they plodded up the stairs to the lunchroom. Muted voices slipped through the half-closed door. When Gibson walked into the room, the talking ceased altogether. He locked eyes with Jason—grey on grey. The chair screeched on the linoleum as he dragged it away from the table and sat down next to Jason. The foreman wiggled in his seat, the hardness pressing into his spine. An offer of coffee from David broke a drawn-out silence. Gibson already had four coffees that morning which was definitely his limit. Not that his hands were shaking but his temper was on edge.

Scottie stuck the fingerprint case on the counter as the crew watched.

"What's going on now?" Jason asked.

"We would like everybody's prints for elimination. If there are no objections," Scottie said, not explaining further.

Nobody objected, although there was some grumbling. Jason stared out the window. Without any hassle, they got the prints done and split down the stairs. David rushed down the steps after them.

"I wanted to tell you about a conference that Robbie and I attended last week. We go every year."

"How will that help us?" Gibson asked.

"One of Robbie's best buddies was there," he said. "He may know something. I should have told you earlier."

"Okay." But it seemed doubtful that anything useful would come out of it.

Chapter 16

After handing off the fingerprint evidence to the constables, Gibson and Scottie stopped to have lunch at a greasy spoon—something they regretted later. They needed to check alibis although everyone had said they had come straight to work at their regular times. Well, who would say otherwise? They would start with Nick. Scottie drove them north a few miles past Cordova Bay to Menawood Place. It was a pretty area with gardens and dense trees bordering the boulevard. The small green bungalow with white trim was tucked behind a towering evergreen hedge. On the paved driveway, someone had parked a black SUV in a haphazard manner as if they had been in a rush. Scottie placed her palm on the hood as they strolled past it.

"It's warm. Somebody's home." They walked down the curved sidewalk to the front door. There was a wooden portico over the stoop that protected people from the outdoor elements. Scottie rapped on a door decorated with carved leaves and flowers. A short woman with mousy brown hair answered. She was wearing a green jacket and brightly coloured scarf. Her makeup did not mask the dark circles under her eyes. Fortunate for them it wouldn't be a wasted trip. Gibson never called ahead. He preferred to keep people on their toes.

"Susan Jones"? Scottie asked, her pleasant grin radiating friendliness.

"Is this about the murder?"

Scottie acknowledged that was the case, a smile lingering on her mouth. She flipped a glance to her partner that silently asked, 'How did we get spotted so easily?'

"But Nick's at work."

"We'd like to speak to you."

Susan's gaze clouded as she glimpsed from one face to the other. She remained rooted in the doorway.

"May we come in for a minute?"

"Sorry. I didn't mean to be rude."

Susan showed them into the living room. It was overcrowded with furniture and knick-knacks but it was exceedingly tidy. Gibson waited for her to sit before selecting his seat. He chose an armchair opposite her and leaned back into the overstuffed chair. Scottie stood near the fireplace with pad and pen at the ready. He started with some general queries to make Susan feel at ease. Did she know the crew at Nick's job? Yes. Did she go to workplace functions? Usually, but missed the celebration on Sunday. Her youngest was ill. Susan sat snugly in the chair with her legs crossed at the ankles. After an exchange of pleasantries, he leaned forward. Now it was time to ask the real questions.

"How close were Nick and Robbie?"

Susan let out a shaky giggle and thrust back into her seat. The question erased her smile. She stared straight ahead, her brown eyes wide open and her lips vanishing as she sucked them inward. She circumvented the question deftly.

"Tim is his best friend at work."

"What time did Nick leave yesterday?" Gibson asked, as if the last answer had satisfied him.

"The normal."

"When would that be?"

"Around six." She hesitated, twirling her wedding ring as she spoke, peering at the promise, 'til death do us part.'

The two detectives glanced at each other.

"Are you sure?"

"No. Like I said, one kid was sick. I was up most the night. Nick was gone by the time I woke up." Her shoulders sagged. "Sorry."

"Okay. We'll be on our way," Gibson said. He stood up to leave.

"Is that all?" Her bewildered expression cut sharp lines on her forehead.

"Yes. Thanks. You've been helpful."

She pulled at her lifeless hair, eyes squeezing shut for a moment.

Scottie put her notebook in a top pocket, and they said their goodbyes. Before the hedge concealed their view, Gibson glanced back to the large bay window. Susan stood behind the sheer drapes scarcely visible. She seemed smaller than when they had first arrived.

"So, what do you think?" Gibson asked. "Nick said he left for work at six-thirty. A half an hour is a long time. Time enough to hit somebody over the head with a bat."

Scottie shrugged.

"She looks worried about something. But about what is another question. Does she think that Nick has something to do with the murder?"

"We should talk to Nick again," Scottie suggested. They leaped into the vehicle and sped to the university.

When they entered the maintenance yard, it looked deserted. Although there were a few cars in the parking lot, all the doors appeared locked. Gibson looked at his watch and realized the day had slipped away. A thundering noise broke the stillness. Nick rushed out the door and halted dead in his tracks.

"What are you doing here?"

"Looking for you," Scottie snarled. "Checking your alibi."

"Why?" Nick asked indignantly. "I didn't do anything."

Scottie pulled out her famous notebook and flipped the sheets. She stared at a page and then scrolled further. She stopped and tapped her pen at a spot on the paper. "You say six-thirty." Then she flicked to the end of her notes. "Your wife says six. Who's lying?" Susan had actually said she thought it was six. But no matter because Nick appeared to be nervous about the question of time. A bead of sweat had formed on his upper lip, and he stood with his feet close together, bouncing from heel to toe. Scottie looked toward the road, and then swung her gaze back to Nick.

"So, what time did you leave for work? Did you get here earlier than you're saying and kill Robbie?"

"No." Nick looked up in alarm.

"Did you see anybody on your way to work that could vouch for you?" Scottie asked. She scribbled in the notebook.

Nick squirmed, his eyes darting back and forth.

"What about Robbie's wife? She's always coming around the yard yelling and screaming about something," he blurted out, seeking to turn the questioning away from him. He nodded his head in satisfaction. "She's crazy enough to do anything. It gets violent."

"Are you saying there was domestic violence?" Gibson tossed a covert glimpse to Scottie.

"Yeah. They're always at odds. Even at our parties. Bickering and…" He paused mid-sentence and squared his shoulders. His feet wouldn't stop bouncing.

"Could one of the other guys verify that?"

"I don't know. Maybe they were breaking up," he said, realizing maybe he had pushed it too far.

"Who else is here?" Gibson switched gears.

"Everybody's gone for the day. Tim left early." The clamour of a bolt slamming against the garage doors caused him to start. "Oh, I forgot about David. He's on lockup duty this week."

"We'll talk again," Gibson said.

Nick jogged toward the parking lot with his backpack bouncing against his shoulder. Gibson watched as he threw the pack into the back seat and fired up the engine. Nick looked straight ahead as he drove past them, turned right and spun his tires to make a clean getaway. As a final squeal of rubber on asphalt faded, David darted out of the building. He issued a short yelp when he saw the detectives, not realizing anybody was there. He locked the door and rattled the knob to ensure it was secure.

"Did you visit Robbie's friend Aaron?" David asked, rolling his neck. They could hear a distinct crack. He grinned.

"Not yet," Gibson said. "Do you have time for a chat?"

David glanced at the vacant parking lot.

"I guess." He flashed a smile. Small wrinkles appeared on the outer side of his eyes as he looked at the detectives. He made a decision to divulge all. So he told them; he told them everything he knew. He described Tim as a bully who made rude jokes, intimidated people by standing close and making inappropriate gestures. Tim's favourite target was Robbie. He pestered and stalked him around the yard. He also tampered with Robbie's belongings and equipment. But Sunday was the first quarrel that had become physical. David staggered back a step to lean against the wall and tilted his head into the structure. The two detectives remained still as they listened to this tale of bullying in the workplace.

"So, what was different?" Gibson asked, although he had a good idea.

"Well, it started when Tim called him Robin," David faltered, maybe doubting giving it all up. But he was tired of keeping it all in, always fearful of the repercussions. And maybe it was Tim who had killed him. So he continued.

"Robbie was dressed as Robin from Batman." He rubbed the back of his neck. "Anyway, he didn't take it this time and called Tim a homo." David clenched his teeth as he went on. "Twink. Robbie screamed out Twink and then all hell broke loose."

Gibson had seen this before. The victim eventually stands up for himself and it turns into a brawl.

"So I wasn't lying. I don't know if Robbie is gay or not." He looked down at his boots and spread out his hands in surrender. "I really don't know. He kept it to himself if he was. But like I told you before, his best friend would know."

"Thanks." Gibson squeezed his shoulder in appreciation and sympathy.

"Sure." David shuffled his feet, his posture wilting. He walked away. Minutes later the jeep roared to life with a sputter and rattle. He waved to them as he pulled into the street, the exhaust rumbling loudly.

"It's been a long day. Let's go home," Gibson said.

They settled in the truck and crawled across town. A growing number of vehicles swarmed around them as they inched their way closer to Brentwood Bay. He flopped back into his seat as Scottie took care of the rush hour traffic.

"I wonder if Ellen realizes how much bullying Robbie put up with at work," he murmured.

A hint of a frown crossed Scottie's face. She had been thinking the same thing.

"This bears all the classic traits of bullies in the workplace. The offensive jokes, the insults, the intimidation. I could go on and on," Gibson continued with his argument. "We really need to take a closer look at Tim."

Scottie didn't comment. She thought the bully factor was there, but had it led to murder? No, she didn't think so. But she let her partner ramble as much as he wanted to and turned up the volume on the radio. Gibson stared out the window. A few trees that still had foliage hanging on the tips of their branches were turning a golden hue. The rain-soaked leaves magnified the brilliance of the sun as it slunk lower in the sky. He realized Katherine hadn't called all day. A tightness in his chest gripped him as his concern heightened. He reached into his back pocket, squirming in the seat to dig out his cell and dialed home, waiting patiently while it rang. After seven rings, he punched the hang-up button and clenched his fist into his mouth. She must be immersed in her studies for the final. He glanced skyward and emitted a long, slow breath.

Chapter 17

After getting dropped off by Scottie, Gibson remained in the driveway for a moment to admire his home. It was a sixties bungalow with a shake roof and weathered wood siding. The trim around the doors and windows was painted a blue-grey. There was just enough colour to give a clean line but also allow the house to fade into the background of greenery. The fir trees towered over the yard, blocking the morning sun. But the westerly view from the front, encompassing the entire bay, made up for the absence of light at the back.

He opened the door to the sound of subdued music floating from the study. After shrugging off his boots, he shuffled along the hallway in his thick woolen socks. He paused momentarily to peek in the room, not wishing to disturb Katherine and her notebooks. She was leaning forward in the chair, left elbow braced on the mahogany desk. The wood had a lovely patina that enriched its warm complexion, the same lustre as the hair spilling over Katherine's arm and brushing the wispy grain. She stared intently at a page packed with columns of numbers. With a coloured pencil in her right hand, she slowly scrolled down the sheet, occasionally making a heavy red check mark on the border. He went through to the kitchen and debated his next move. An easy decision. Off to the café. Then a spin around the bay. He changed into his boating attire and made his getaway through the back door.

The Seaside Cafe was gearing down for the day, but he spotted his good buddy sitting beside the window that hung over the water—Gibson's favourite spot. Jesse Players was looking beyond the boats, kayaks and canoes lying on the wooden dock. His gaze sought the ocean sparkling in the sunlight. Ripples formed on the surface by a gentle breeze. A mug of coffee cupped in his hands was almost empty.

"Hey."

"Have you got time for a drink before you go out in your kayak?" Jesse asked with a grin.

"You bet." Gibson snorted. Jesse had him pegged. He pulled out a chair at the end of the table and sat down.

The waitress came hurrying over with a pot of coffee. She leaned against the table top with her hip and ventured a guess.

"Coffee?"

"Please."

Gibson sat back and smiled at his buddy. The men had been friends back east. Jesse had moved here years before, and they had lost touch. Gibson had been on a solitary stroll when they bumped into each other on the waterfront path. It was a nice surprise for both men. As they became reacquainted it was clear they had lots in common. Hardly a week passed by and they could be seen in serious discussion at this same table, chatting for hours. It was developing into a strong friendship.

Jesse had worked in investment banking on the Niagara Peninsula before retiring to the west coast. He no longer dressed in tailored suits or sported short business-style hair. Now he wore jeans and chunky sweaters. His cropped hair had grown into a brown wavy mane that touched the top of his rumpled shirt collar. And the polished Italian shoes were exchanged for well-worn sneakers. Despite an acrimonious divorce, a playful smile was still planted on his face. His soft hands had turned hard and calloused from outdoor play. His days were occupied with kayaking, hikes and to slow it down a bit, some reading. He volunteered at the university in the business department as a mentor. Occasionally he helped Katherine with her studies by coaching her in his area of expertise.

Gibson captivated his buddy with some of his more compelling cases—with discretion. He figured this was one of them and was curious about Jesse's perception of the murder. He summarized a skimpier version of the facts so far, of which there were few.

Jesse directed his gaze back to the sea watching the blues and greens of the incessantly flowing water dance with the light.

"Someone who commits a hate crime is prejudiced toward another individual for lots of reasons. Race and religion come to mind. This crime does appear to be against a person's sexual orientation."

"Okay."

"Or the killer's belief that this person was gay," Jesse said. His gaze was concentrated at a spot halfway to the window, making his eyes appear crossed. His eyebrows gathered together in contemplation. "If it is a hate crime, that is. You're the detective."

Gibson's ears picked up this last remark, paying no heed to the dig. Jesse's divergent interpretations always entertained. He pondered the prospect that the killer just assumed his victim was gay. An alternative take on the issue. That's why he liked meeting with him. He mulled over his friend's opinion about this being a hate crime or not. He was convinced it still was.

"See you later." Jesse stood up, rapped his knuckles on the table and took off for home.

Although Gibson would pass this new concept by Scottie, he wasn't sure it made a real difference. Being gay or not could be irrelevant. People often detest things they perceive are truths even when they are lies. He tapped a finger against his lips thinking everything through. Other motives needed to be explored too. He decided not to get fixated in one direction and push away his preconceived theory about this crime. That path could muddy the waters. But it was hard to maintain an impartial mind when he thought of that little shit, Tim. He rattled his brain to knock out the internal conversation. His coffee had become cold. He glanced up at the clock, paid his tab and trekked down the dock to drop his boat in the water. He paddled in and out of different nooks enjoying his freedom. An hour had gone by and the light had faded. A sudden shadow was cast over him and his kayak. He looked over to the western horizon and realized the sun had dropped below the ridge of mountains. Time to get back.

* * *

Katherine was still hunkered over the scattered books on the desktop, pencil in hand. Her elbow was in the same position as before, but now it sagged a little lower. Gibson crept by and stepped into the kitchen. Crushed green peppercorn emanated from the oven. He opened the door to investigate. The aroma of shepherd's pie assailed him along with a blast of heat. His mouth watered, and he felt pangs of hunger rumble in his belly. He slipped into the study, approached his wife, leaning over to lay an affectionate kiss on her already puckered lips. He received a warm welcome.

Gibson came up for air.

"I'm ravenous."

Katherine's face lit up with pleasure.

"The pie."

She jabbed him in the arm with her pencil, and they headed to the kitchen. Gibson got out the wine glasses while she filled their plates to overflowing and a salad on the side. They sat at the oval table and dug in. Andrew, Heather and Scottie's current girlfriend were the subjects of their gossip.

"Heather has a thing for Andrew, but…" She stalled, fumbling for words.

"That's women's business," Gibson said and held up a palm to ward off love talk.

Katherine propped her chin up with a hand and chuckled. It was a comfortable meal with scrumptious food, a red wine from the Okanagan and a wife who seemed relaxed. After dinner, Gibson whistled while he loaded the dirty dishes in the sink. Katherine retreated to her study. She closed the door behind her, blocking out anymore distractions.

Depleted from the day, Gibson went to bed. The warm quilt was comforting as he nestled into its folds, shielding him like a silken cocoon. His head dropped to the pillow, and he dreamed of mountains and water. And his kayak.

* * *

Unbeknownst to Gibson during the wee hours of the morning, two patrolmen were dispatched to investigate a commotion at the university near the unsanctioned camp. A homeless man had been severely beaten, the caller said. By the time the officers arrived, most of the campers had dispersed. They took what witness statements they could, then left to write up their report.

Chapter 18

Gibson's lean figure was silhouetted against the rays streaming through the tinted window. The intensity of the November sun all but obliterated the hint of grey in his sandy hair. There was a power in his tall posture. A suggestion of resolve played across his smooth-shaven face. His stare was set on the opposite wall, not discerning his surroundings. A wandering cloud blocked the light momentarily. He shifted his gaze toward the intrusion on his reverie. The billowy mass scurried off, returning brilliance to the room. Instantly he closed his eyes against the onslaught and turned away.

The office had been quiet all morning. Most of the detectives were on assignment or active with separate cases. He could hear someone across the hallway shouting down a phone. Probably Gunner. After a short time, he gradually opened his eyes again, adjusting to the elevated level of brightness. He saw Scottie standing at the entrance, reluctant to break his meditation. She had a paper clutched securely in one fist and a bag in the other. Abruptly he moved from the window and sat behind the desk. With an elbow resting on the surface, he unconsciously rubbed at his crooked nose. His partner moved into the room.

"What's that?" Gibson pointed to the scraps of paper. With a wave of his palm, he gestured for Scottie to sit.

"The name and address of Robbie's friend from the conference." She raised her hand. "And coffee." She grinned and dropped heavily in the leather-clad chair. She took two lattes and two cinnamon buns from the sack, placing them on the desk. He raised his eyebrows but didn't make a move forward. Instead, he pulled out the lower drawer and propped his feet on the corner. Then he slumped further into his seat, crossing his arms over his chest. He ran his fingers through his hair and fiddled with his collar. Scottie pushed a coffee and bun within Gibson's reach.

"How's that for service?" She chuckled.

They were content to sit in silence and enjoy their snack. Scottie leaned back. She watched the patterns of light ricocheting off the bird prints mounted in thick silver frames and figured it was Heather's artwork. The pinpricks of brightness flickered rapidly around the office like a strobe in a darkened nightclub.

"We have found no reason for someone to want Robbie dead." She searched Gibson's charcoal eyes waiting for the rebuttal. It came swiftly.

"Hate crime," Gibson retorted, thrusting his chin upwards in self-righteousness. Then he lowered his chin almost as fast. He had pledged yesterday he would maintain an open mind. Oh well! But what did they know for certain? It was time to review what they knew. Robbie had biked to work. He had been struck on the back of his skull. With a bat. Probably kneeling down to tie a loose shoelace. He quarrelled with his spouse regularly. Everyone in the maintenance division was either a bully or was bullied. Two witnesses may or may not have seen something.

Not much of anything.

Scottie put both elbows on the desk and interlaced her hands. Gibson pitched his empty paper cup in the trash basket. He wiped the crumbs off the surface into his palm and tossed them in too. Then he thought of another possibility.

"What's Nick up to? He was shaken up when he saw the condom. Was he involved with Robbie sexually?" He stopped and let this idea whirl around in his mind. "Without passing judgement, Nick's wife is so, so." He gestured his hand, side to side. What did he mean by that? A husband would cheat on his spouse because she was plain looking? With another guy? He was losing it.

Scottie shifted her weight in the chair, her backside numb from sitting still and uncomfortable with those kinds of thoughts.

"Let's go for a ride," Gibson said as he pushed himself to his feet.

They set off in Scottie's vehicle, heading east to the Rockland area. The streets criss-crossed at random and changed names at district lines making navigation difficult. At last they drew up to their destination. It was a substantial two-storey mansion built in the 1900s, a fine example of the Arts and Crafts architectural style. Samuel Maclure, he concluded. A cross-gabled roof with flaring eaves, a gable dormer, exposed soffits and double-hung leaded-glass windows dominated the design. The detailing was amazing with decorative tooth-like dentils on the fascia boards and large stones circling the foundation. The cladding was a combination of cedar shingles and narrower lap siding.

The detectives admired the house before they walked up the broad stairs leading to the veranda. It was framed by great square posts. The solid red oak door had recessed panels with clear bevelled glass inserted at the top. Once upon a time, this dwelling had been a private family residence. Now three bells were lined up beside the glass. Alongside each was a handwritten name inserted into a decorative brass plate. The first bell was labelled 'A. Fraser', the individual they were seeking. As soon as Gibson pressed the buzzer, the door swung open. A young man rigged out in a leather jacket with a red wool scarf hanging loosely from his neck almost ran into him. He had tousled brown hair and a dark bushy moustache that drooped down the edges of his mouth. At the moment, it was turned down in a gruff scowl.

"Aaron Fraser?" Gibson asked.

"Yes. Who are you?" He took a step forward but neither of the detectives made any effort to move aside.

"We're with the major crime unit. May we speak to you for a moment?"

They both flashed their badges.

"I was just heading back to work," Aaron said. He glanced at his watch and pursed his mouth disapprovingly. "What is this about?"

"Do you know Robbie Spencer?"

"Yes. Robbie is a good friend." Aaron froze. "Has something happened?"

"Robbie was murdered."

He bent over as if he had taken a bullet in the gut.

"Oh my god." He covered his mouth with both hands and closed his eyes. "I saw him last week." He paused and sucked in some air. "I can't believe this."

Setting a hand on Aaron's arm, Gibson guided him inside. The entrance opened directly into a room as beautiful as the exterior. A massive fireplace with an extensive oak timber on top extended out two feet and overshadowed the entire space. The gilded mirror above it looked as if it had hung in a castle from the last century. The mantel was loaded with photos in metal frames. A jeweled chandelier left behind from glorious days hung to the side, misplaced by the partitioning of the house. The furnishings were masculine, simple and elegant.

Aaron flopped heavily into an armchair by the door. His head fell against the velvet brocade. The golden threads of the rich woven fabric picked up the light above his head. Gibson chose a seat across from him and rested his palms on his thighs. Scottie stood close to the hearth and scrutinized the faces in the snapshots.

"Who? Why?" He lifted his head and looked over to Gibson. His brown eyes had welled up with tears. He coughed to clear his throat and hold off his despair.

Gibson told him what had happened at the yard, trying to keep out the gory details. The glow on Aaron's cheeks faded to an ashen hue. He clamped his hands into a death grip and held them on his lap. When Gibson suggested that Robbie was gay, he protested.

"No way!" Aaron sprung forward, but a look of doubt had washed over his features. He rested back, his hands clasped in prayer now and pressed to his mouth. "Maybe."

Gibson believed the pain on Aaron's face was real and gave him time to centre himself. After a moment he continued and told him that bullying seemed to be prominent at Robbie's workplace. Aaron released a heavy sigh and let all his anger out in a shaking, rage-filled voice.

"No kidding. They pestered him relentlessly. If it wasn't the bike shorts, it was his bone structure or his high-pitched voice. They clutched at anything to bring the guy down. He's my best friend." He pounded his fist on the arm of his chair. "The bastards."

"We don't know who did this yet or the reason," Scottie said. She threw an annoying sideways glance to Gibson. "Have you noticed any changes with Robbie?"

Gibson could see Aaron working something out in his mind, so he kept quiet.

"There is something that's been bothering me. Not sure if it's relevant though." He blew out some air. "He's been spending a lot of money. Fixing up his car. Trips. Stuff like that." He paused. "Although he was getting an inheritance from his dad who died recently. Maybe he already got it so I'm blowing smoke here. It's probably nothing."

"Every bit of information helps." Gibson stood up to leave. "Sorry for your loss. Take care." He looked back before he closed the door. Aaron's face seemed to slacken as he sunk into his grief. There was a rawness to the tears that rolled down his cheek.

They walked down the sidewalk to the truck.

"Money could be an issue here. Aaron noticed a change in his habits," Scottie said.

"Yeah."

"Gunner and Na are already checking finances. Should we see what they've found out so far? We should tell them what we just heard about the excess spending."

"Sure." Gibson leaned on the roof of the vehicle and nodded in agreement. Could be something there. Or not.

* * *

Getting from Rockland through downtown to Dallas Road took Scottie twenty minutes. Gibson sat in the passenger seat with his legs thrust out. He liked being chauffeured around town as much as she enjoyed driving. As they rounded the corner to the office, sunlight flowed through the windshield and struck his face. How long this dry spell would last was anybody's guess, Gibson thought, as he reveled in the caress of the sun. November on the coast usually comprised of heavy rains and strong winds. It was coming. Just enjoy the reprieve from the imminent fall storms.

They parked on the street and entered the building through the hefty glass doors. He wasn't sure if they were bulletproof, but they were thick and mirrored and kept stray eyes from snooping. This time the receptionist was on duty. She smiled pleasantly, her bright white teeth on full display. Although she recognized them by sight, it was protocol to log the comings and goings of all staff during office hours. On the off hours, the place was locked up tight with only a few having access to the electronic keypad.

They crossed the marble floors to the staircase, heels clomping on the spotless surface. Not a lot of civilian traffic got much farther than here. Up the stairs their footfalls echoed even louder. Gibson peered into the front offices as they passed by. Gunner was nowhere in sight. Probably in the can. Na was leaning forward in his chair, elbows on his desk and cell phone pinned to his ear. He held up one finger to let them know he was almost finished. They sat down to wait it out. Gunner bounced into the room.

"Hey, I was looking for you guys. I found a photo on Robbie's Facebook," he said.

Gibson waited.

"It's Robbie with some guy. You decide." He pulled a copy of the picture from his desk drawer and handed it over to Gibson. Scottie peeked over his arm.

Robbie's face was unmistakable. The other person had twisted away and was in motion causing the features to blur.

"It might come in handy later. Thanks." He pocketed the photo.

Na bobbed his head one last time and placed his cell on the files strewn over the desk. He grinned, all fired up to report his news.

"It makes sense that Ellen is in the will. Right?" Na said, getting straight into the nitty-gritty. "But get this, Jeff is too."

From the corner of the room, they could hear a printer churning out page after page. Na walked over and gathered the sheets together. He passed them all to Gibson.

"Here's a copy of the will."

Scottie slid her chair in closer to get a better look.

"Really. Why would that be, I wonder?"

"Back to Cadboro Bay?" Gibson stared at Scottie with upraised eyebrows. They hustled out of the office with a fast-paced strut in search of definitive answers.

"How much money are we talking here?" Scottie muttered under her breath as they scampered down the stairs. An unexpected blast of cold air bombarded them when they opened the glass doors. Dark clouds high in the sky were rushing in from the Northeast. A change was coming sooner rather than later. Gibson tugged at his jacket to secure it against the squall and dashed to the truck.

Scottie powered through Fairfield, down Foul Bay Road and skipped over a few streets to Henderson. This time Ellen responded to the summons of the buzzer. She was in her pyjamas, eyes swollen and red. Wearily she trudged down the hallway to the kitchen. Cheerfulness had permanently fled the home. No sweet scent of sugar and cinnamon infused the room. Lily sat in a highchair tossing cereal on the ground, unusually subdued. No running, jumping or dancing going on today. Not even the appearance of visitors swayed the little girl into action. Without question, she felt her mother's sombre demeanour and some basic instinct kept her still.

Gibson drew a chair away from the table and perched himself on the edge. Meanwhile, Scottie took her stand as sentinel inconspicuously against a wall. Ellen picked up Fruity O's off the floor, her loss of interest showing on her face, until he asked about the will.

"What about the will?" The darkness in her eyes spread over her face.

"Why was Jeff in it?" Gibson asked again, not answering her concerns but intent on a response.

"Hang on." Ellen plucked Lily from her chair and left the kitchen with her child propped on her hip. A few minutes passed by and they could hear a cartoon playing in the living room. She returned empty handed. A crunch sounded under her slipper as she walked past the high chair. She cast her eyes around the disorder of her more often than not welcoming kitchen. The dishes had piled up by the sink, mostly mugs and soup bowls. Gibson could tell by the slow blinking of her eyelids that her thoughts tumbled in a frenzy. The wall clock ticked by slowly as they waited for her to find a way forward. She ran her fingers absently along the table top.

"Robbie was a good man." She stopped and looked up at him. "But we all do stupid things we regret. Don't we?"

Gibson nodded.

"He cheated Jeff, but he was ashamed of it."

She clutched the edge of the table so tightly that Gibson could feel her hand vibrating through the wood. Scottie remained in the corner of the room, trying to be invisible.

"Robbie and Jeff had the same mother who had promised both brothers would be taken care of after she died. But Robbie's father didn't feel the same. She passed away before him, and the estate went to his only real son, Robbie." Her shoulders trembled, the tension in her muscles tightening more. She continued. "The dispute was bitter. Robbie felt the money belonged to him and told his half-brother to take a hike. He wouldn't share."

Gibson nodded once more.

"But remorse hit Robbie hard. It wasn't in his DNA to be that mean. That's why Jeff is in the will. He wanted to make up for his actions."

"Does Jeff know all this?" Gibson tilted forward.

"Yeah, he does."

Gibson exchanged a look with Scottie.

"What about your fights?"

His cell rang.

"Damn." Gibson held up his hand and left the room. After a minute he returned.

"Sorry. Go on. The fights."

"Somebody's been telling tales out of school." Ellen frowned. "It wasn't that big of a deal. It was about the kids. Robbie had his own views on how things should work." She stopped and tugged nervously at her greasy hair. "Sometimes it got out of hand. I don't know why I went to the shop. That was my stupidity."

"Okay."

"Now he's gone." The worries of yesterday disappeared when the worries of tomorrow and the next day came to her mind. "What will I do?"

"Do you want us to call someone for you?" He launched himself to his feet and indicated to Scottie it was time to go.

She shook her head half-heartedly.

"You take care." There wasn't much else Gibson could say. It was always the same. The grief would come in waves. Some would overwhelm and knock you down; some would be a comforting blanket. He peeked into the living room before leaving. Lily sat cross-legged in front of the blaring television. She looked at him with questioning eyes, the loss not reaching her young thoughts yet. She had her mom all to herself.

"That was Officer Eddy Evans," Gibson said as they ambled down the walkway.

"I like him."

"One of the homeless guys got beaten up last night. We better check it out."

"Do you want to ask around the neighbourhood before we take off?" Scottie asked. She pointed to a particular house.

"What are you thinking?"

"Neighbours can be nosy. Maybe someone saw something?"

"Like what?"

"Did Ellen go out early that morning?"

"I don't think..."

"Probably not. But best to make sure."

"Okay. Then we'll go to the camp."

* * *

The house across the street had a large bay window, and most likely a clear view of the house opposite—Robbie and Ellen's home. A short older lady answered the bell almost immediately as if she had been on Neighbourhood Watch.

"Come in, come in." She fluttered her hands in the air. The luminous skin was wrinkled and paper thin with blotches of brown. Her silver-grey hair was thinning in spots and revealed a bright pink scalp. The green and blue flowered dress was belted at the middle where her waist should have been.

They showed her their badges, but this lady knew who they were.

"Should I go over there?" She had heard about Robbie's death on the radio and wasn't sure what to do. Her eyes bugged out. Gibson guessed it was more from curiosity than from fear.

"Yes. You should," he said. "She's pretty shaken up."

"No doubt Ellen will be very upset."

"Did you see her that morning?"

"Yes, I'm an early riser. Ellen picks up the paper every morning. The paperboy tosses it up on the porch. Sometimes it doesn't make it all the way. Terrible."

"What time would that be?"

"Quarter after six."

"Did Ellen go out on Monday?"

"Her car was in the driveway all morning," she said and flushed with sudden embarrassment. "I notice things like that..." She trailed off.

Probably because you are a nosy parker, Gibson thought. He looked out the window. The glass was spotless and in a direct line to the front door across the street.

"So, do Robbie and Ellen get along?"

The old lady narrowed her eyes and glared intently at him with her hawkish look.

"It's none of my business, but I wasn't aware of any trouble." She puckered her lips. All the goodwill had disappeared from her face.

They thanked her and left precipitously.

"Yikes," Scottie said. "Any reason to check other neighbours?"

"I don't think so."

They walked away from the house and hopped into the truck. Scottie fired up the engine and headed down Henderson. She took the university circle road to the homeless camp. As she drove, her fingers lightly skimmed the steering wheel.

"It doesn't seem like Ellen had anything to do with Robbie's death."

"Without meaning to sound sexist, I don't think this was a woman's crime," Gibson said. He blushed somewhat. "What can I say?" He shot her a sideways glance.

Scottie grinned at his discomfort but conceded the killer was probably a man. It would take a strong person to swing that bat and produce that much harm, although she would be capable of just that.

"Jeff is a hefty guy but on the short side." Then after a moment she added, "Guess that wouldn't matter. The ME said that Robbie may have been tying his shoelaces."

"There's that."

"And he has a compelling motive. Money."

"Maybe so."

Scottie parked the truck on the street by the university, and they strolled across the expansive lawn. Although it was green, the autumn rains had made the ground soggy. As Gibson stepped around the waterlogged bits, he realized the light had dimmed considerably since morning. He peered up and saw the clouds had blackened and were closing in to create one ominous mass.

An assortment of cans, empty cigarette packages and debris littered the path leading through the bushes. As they approached the clearing partially hidden by a large willow tree, they could see a circle of mates smoking and chatting. The men were seated on rotted stumps and makeshift chairs made from wooden boxes. The first rustle of branches pushed aside alerted them, and all talk ceased. The detectives stepped into the open space, two imposing figures with the air of authority swirling around them.

"It's okay. We're not here to hassle anybody. Who got beat up last night?"

No reply.

"What's it to you?" someone shouted in a gruff voice.

"Was it Pete? We talked to him about the murder already."

"Yeah. But he's missing," a man in a tattered shirt answered.

"Missing?"

"Yeah. Gone," another snickered.

Gibson tugged at Scottie's sleeve to signal the futility of talking to these guys. They wouldn't be opening up any time soon to the police. They headed back to the vehicle.

"Did the guy see something?"

"Don't know. Nobody's telling," Gibson answered, exasperated at the lack of cooperation from Pete's buddies. His cell buzzed as they pulled up to Jeff's driveway. "Okay. Yes." He rang off.

"Well. What?"

"We got ID on the prints from the bat," Gibson said. "Robbie, Tim, one unknown and our friend Jeff."

"Two strikes," Scottie said. She pressed the bell, leaning into it hard.

"What the hell?" Jeff appeared at the door dressed in sweatpants and a T-shirt. His hair looked clean and combed today. He turned toward the living room, and they followed him. It was smoky as ever. Scottie clamped her mouth shut. They stood in a semi-circle prepared to spar.

"Is the bat yours?" Gibson snapped, ready to strike the first blow.

"Okay. You got me. It's my bat. Those are my initials." Jeff sneered.

"Your prints are on it as well." That was really a moot point.

"So what! I lent it to Robbie last week."

"Why did you lie to us?"

"I didn't want to get involved."

"You know you're in Robbie's will to inherit a nice chunk of cash."

"Good. I'm broke."

"Ellen told us you already knew," Gibson countered.

Jeff looked back at him with narrowed eyes, not prepared to admit anything.

"And you have no one to establish your whereabouts Monday morning?"

"How could I? I live alone," Jeff repeated. He backed away in quick jerky steps.

"One, your bat. Two, get money. Three, no alibi." Scottie numbered off on her fingers, staring squarely into Jeff's eyes, one brown, one blue—heterochromia.

Then they heard the rain hit the roof with a deafening outburst.

Chapter 19

The ride home couldn't have been much more treacherous. Heavy rainfall and wind with gusts up to sixty kilometres blew against the windshield, making visibility almost non-existent. Scottie gripped the steering wheel firmly with both hands, tilted forward toward the glass. Each swipe of the wipers cleared the view for only seconds. She peered ahead with eyes squinted, a large frown encasing her face. Gibson maintained a lookout for dashing pedestrians and bicycles fighting the storm. Soon they were on the freeway. Water surging down the hard surface made the roads slick. Several times they sped through puddles pooled in low spots, shooting a rooster tail tumbling over the vehicle behind them. They got nailed with a few themselves, offering a fleeting glimpse of driving underwater.

"Thanks for running me around while my truck was getting repaired," Gibson said when they arrived at the garage in Brentwood Bay.

"No problem," Scottie replied and drove off.

After a brief chat with the mechanic, Gibson got into his F150 and motored on home. The sheets of rain had tamed down to a drizzle, and then stopped by the time he parked in his driveway. A pool of white light lapped around the lamp. He looked across the street. Sea smoke that develops when frigid air passes over warm water obscured the bay. The fog rested only ten metres above the surface, allowing the cell tower beacon on the Malahat to glow through. He watched, mesmerized by the swirls of mist dancing in the cove. Then he realized how late it was and tore from his trance.

"Hello," he shouted out for Katherine as he tripped into the house.

She tiptoed out of the kitchen looking frazzled. He saw the characteristic display of panic. The ragged breathing, the black shadows beneath the eyes and the collapsed stance were all present.

"How did the studying go today?"

"Okay, I guess." She rested against the doorframe with one foot planted on top of the other. Her hair tumbled forward partially covering her face.

He reached over and placed his hand under her chin, lifting gently until their eyes engaged, her dark chocolate brown to his deep charcoal.

"We're meeting Andrew in an hour. The break will do you good," he said.

"Can't we cancel? The final exam is just days away."

To Katherine, graduating seemed the only way to quell her fears—her attacks.

Gibson saw the tension in her shoulders and her shallow breathing quicken.

"I'm buying." Just a tickle of silliness.

A tiniest of smiles twitched at the corner of her mouth. She tried to suppress it with her hand. She pressed into him, lips brushed against his neck. He tightened his hold on her slender frame. They remained embraced for several minutes. He could sense her body release as her unease subsided. Her softness against the strength of his chest was intoxicating. They drew apart and gazed at each other. They dropped hands, and he stroked her hair.

"Better get moving before I run into trouble." Gibson lifted his eyebrows suggestively. 'You know what I mean.'

The grin that had begun at Katherine's mouth reached upwards and created small creases in the outer corners of her eyes, making them sparkle.

They touched fingertips one more time.

"Should we get ready then?"

They stepped out the front door and clambered into the F150. Dense clouds overshadowed the sky, giving only brief glimpses of the moon. It was still early evening and growing chilly. Katherine pulled her woolly coat firmly around her slim body. The traffic was thin as they cruised down the highway to Oak Bay. Soft music filled the cab, blending with the rhythmic percussion of the tires. Gibson parked on Beach Street, and they strode down the pavement holding hands.

* * *

The Cove Pub in the Ocean Tides Hotel was Andrew's favourite inn—fish and chips, beer on tap and expansive vistas. Harris Island and the Chain Islets were easily viewed through the large windows. Andrew enjoyed it all while he sipped his brew and waited for the gang to arrive. From his booth, he could see the lighthouse beacon on Discovery Island. It swept a light at regular intervals across the ocean waters and marked the border between Canada and the United States. The Marine Provincial Park was on this isle. The adjacent islands were part of the ecological reserve that preserved the sensitive seabird nesting areas. Boaters paddled along the shoreline, respecting the biological diversity of the west coast. They were eager to capture a glimpse of seals, sea lions and bald eagles. He knew Gibson kayaked throughout here frequently.

He spotted his sister as soon as she entered the room. Shiny cascades of coffee brown hair tumbled over a bronze scarf wrapped around the upturned collar and onto her shoulders. The dark pencil skirt and alligator shoes with tall, thin heels portrayed a strong, confident woman. But Katherine's compressed lips betrayed her frailty, her uneasiness. He recognized this in her when most would not. He thought people would notice only her physical allure and the elegance of her spirit that radiated through her soulful eyes. She was damaged inside.

Gibson placed his palm on Katherine's elbow and guided them through the narrow aisles to the booth. He drew his fair share of attention too. The crisp white shirt under a baby blue cashmere sweater and tight black jeans spoke smart and easygoing. His bent nose and the quirky smile added to his mystique, noticeably to the fairer sex. They presented an image of the ideal couple.

Andrew watched as they approached the booth. His sagacity of human behaviour made him aware that we all had flaws. He wondered if Gibson's veneer of serenity would break down. So far none had surfaced from his genial although solemn disposition.

"Hello, my favourite people," Andrew greeted them. The clean-shaven face didn't betray his profession but the tweed jacket and wool trousers did. His thick, stocky build and chiselled chin emanated a power of position, but his cheery demeanour softened the harshness to one of trust.

"Hello, my beloved brother," Katherine said.

They ordered fish and chips and drinks and settled into the plump cushions.

"This is awesome," Katherine said as she delved into the salted fries.

Good food, good mood. Gibson wanted to hang onto this time, knowing her need to feel normal.

Andrew squirmed in his seat. He had something to say but didn't know how to. A tiny bead of perspiration rolled down the side of his face.

"Anybody for dessert?" His courage had deserted him.

Everyone refused. The conversation shifted to local events with Heather's art show topping the list. Gibson scanned the room after ordering a coffee. Partly obscured behind a screen, he spotted his partner. Scottie and her companion were snuggled close, gazing into each other's eyes.

"We have lovebirds," Gibson said as he pointed toward the corner cubicle. "Are they trying to hide from us? Be right back."

Scottie was dressed in a green and black plaid flannel blouse and jeans. Her dainty girlfriend had on a royal blue turtleneck sweater with grey wool slacks. A delicate gold locket hung from a slim chain, highlighting her elfin features. Sherry shrieked with delight when he sat next to her. She tipped forward and pecked his cheek.

Andrew thought this was his opportunity. He dreaded divulging his secrets to Gibson. Did he have the heart to encumber his sister with his problem? Would Katherine empathize with him or turn aside? Too late. Gibson strolled back.

Chapter 20

Not a speck of blue sky was visible through the cloud cover. A mass of whiteness hung low, covering the mountain range across the strait, leaving just snow-dusted tops peeking out. Wispy clouds swept down to the chilly ocean water, hovering feet above the continuous turbulent motion—the tide was pushing upstream. The dullness of the atmosphere made the morning seem like twilight, matching Gibson's sullen mood as he stared out the window.

"Hey," Scottie greeted him as she wandered into the office. "You're in early today."

Gibson turned around with a scowl planted solidly in place.

"Sure is depressing," he said and flung his hands up. "This time of year."

Scottie stayed and waited for him to speak further.

"At least it's not raining or snowing. Let's find Tim." His quirky smile made an appearance. "That will make me feel better."

"You bet."

She drove them through rush hour traffic with a proficiency that was impressive, showing up at the maintenance sheds in record time. She pulled to the curb with a jerk. They jumped out of the vehicle just as David rounded the corner of the building.

David spotted them and spun around instantaneously, not skipping a beat. Gibson caught the motion at the edge of his vision.

"Hey, David. Stop. Can we talk?"

He halted mid-stride, turned and walked back.

"Yeah, what's up?" His body was rigid, lips forming a slash across his face. His eyes were hooded as if he was hiding from something.

"You know more about Robbie than you're letting on." Gibson went with his instincts.

"What do you mean?" David closed his hands by his side, creating tight fists.

"That he was gay."

"No. But I can tell you that Robbie and Nick had a quarrel a few weeks ago." He furrowed his eyebrows and made his decision. "It could have been a lover's squabble."

"What made you think that?"

"It just looked chummy. Ask Nick. I got to go." He let out the deepest of sighs.

"Thanks." Gibson shifted his eyes to Scottie again.

David scurried out of the courtyard with the detectives looking after him.

"What was that?"

"Who knows? Maybe something. Maybe nothing at all," Gibson mumbled under his breath.

They took an about turn and walked to the garage in silence. The place seemed deserted so they stomped up the stairs to check it out. Jason's door was closed and the glass transom above it showed no light. They swung left into the lunchroom. Tim was at the table sipping a coffee and texting. He glimpsed slyly from the corner of his eye and grumbled.

"You guys again." Tim looked every bit the bully with his menacing look. His direct penetrating blue eyes were unnerving.

Scottie remained static with her arms crossed over her chest, an intimidating smirk curling her lips. Gibson strolled to the centre of the room and halted, slamming his notebook on the counter. He stood hands on his hips, his large presence hovering over Tim.

"What do you want?" Tim shoved his chair back, making it screech on the linoleum floor.

"We want some answers."

"What?" Tim extended his legs and clasped both hands behind his neck.

"That's right. What are your prints doing on the bat?" Gibson asked sharply as he settled himself on a wobbly bench opposite him. He then continued, "The bat you know nothing about. Never seen it before." He dragged out the final phrase.

"I knew it. You're trying to fix this on me." He jumped to his feet.

Gibson glanced over to Scottie blocking any escape. But as swiftly as Tim had surged up, he plunged back into his chair.

"Look, you guys. I was just goofing around in the parking lot. Punching rocks into the hedge." The bluster had taken a back seat.

"Why would you do that?"

"Just for fun."

Gibson smelt a whiff of fear radiate from the bully.

"Look. Robbie left it here. That's all. I didn't hit him." He quit chatting and stared at the floor. "This is absurd."

Tension drove most people to reveal, so Gibson sat still and waited it out. Scottie was scribbling in her notebook, the scratching noise of pen on paper audible in the quietness. Tim fidgeted, shifting his weight and shuffling his feet under his chair. He coughed, licked his parched lips and said more.

"I figure it's his brother's bat. Or I suppose Jeff's his half-brother." Tim exhaled anew, sweat popping up on his forehead. He swiped it off with his shirt sleeve. Anxiety kept him babbling. "I saw Jeff at the shop last week talking to Robbie. He was twirling a bat, and later he tossed it at the back of the shop. So I figured it was okay to use it. Robbie was at a conference. No big deal."

Gibson thought he had just said the same thing another way.

"Can anyone vouch for your whereabouts on Monday morning?" Gibson asked, shifting gears.

"Not really." He screwed up his eyes. "The wife is in the hospital. So I'm on my own. I left at six thirty. Came straight here."

Gibson didn't remark on that. They had already found out where his spouse was, and she wouldn't be his alibi. It was ironic that a nice girl like her would marry a bully.

Just as he was moving to pack it in, Gibson received a call from forensics.

"Hey, Jocko. What have you got for me?" His expression changed from interested to concern. "Okay. Thanks." After he hung up, he turned to Tim. "Where is Nick working?"

"At the rink. Are we done here?"

"Sure."

Gibson wanted to flip the creep a finger, but he held back. They raced down the stairs and out the door.

"What did Jocko find?" She took a fleeting look over to him as they hurried across the yard.

"A print on the condom box."

"Oh yeah."

"Yup. And the condom in question is the same brand as the box."

"Guess somebody got careless." Scottie raised her eyebrows. "Wiped the prints from the foil on the condom and forgot about the box. Good for us." She waited for Gibson to say more.

"They're Nick's prints."

"Holy shit!" Scottie exclaimed, surprise lighting up her face. They left the vehicle parked on the street and tramped across the boulevard and over the sprawling lawns to the arena. A side gate was unlocked so they stole their way into the building. They heard the rumble of a Zamboni. Nick was perched high in the seat, hanging onto the wheel tightly. He steered it through the corners with expert skill. The detectives lingered on the bleachers rubbing their palms together to keep warm. Nick spotted them and moaned. Then he held up an index finger to let them know he was nearly done. The Zamboni had shaved off the top ice, leaving behind a layer of fresh water. It made the surface look wet and shiny. After ten minutes he strolled up the aisle and sat down on a bleacher below them.

"What's going on?"

"We found a condom box in the lunchroom garbage can. Your prints were on it." He searched Nick for a reaction. Not a flinch.

"Same brand as the one under Robbie," Gibson said, so as to make it perfectly clear where he was going with this.

Nick blanched but disclosed nothing, his eyes roving around the rink. A lengthy silence ensued as Gibson waited for a response. None materialized.

"Can you explain that?"

Still Nick scanned for an answer. He rested heavily in his seat causing the bench to creak with protest. Another long hush permeated the arena.

"If you don't tell us, we'll bring you downtown—" Annoyance resonated through his words.

"It's personal."

"This is an investigation. So give it up."

"Oh god. I brought a lady upstairs after the party. You know…for sex." Nick paused. "But nothing happened. I just chucked everything in the garbage. It was stupid." He tapped his fingers on the back of the chair in a relentless rhythm.

"What's the woman's name?" Gibson knew that Nick was the lockup guy that night—last man out.

"Kim. I can't remember her surname."

"You're cheating on your spouse with a stranger?" Scottie asked. Her expression had changed from scepticism to incredulity as she listened to Nick's explanation.

"I didn't cheat."

"We want confirmation on this, Nick," Gibson said. "We need to speak to this Kim person. The sooner the better. Is that clear?"

"Okay. I'll get it. Don't worry. I don't understand how the condom landed up under Robbie. I didn't put it there. I didn't kill him."

"Are you involved somehow?" Gibson's eyes had gone cold. Nick may or may not be the killer, but he might be mixed up in other ways.

"No!" Nick protested, gripping the seat until his knuckles turned white.

"Then tell us about the gay bashing." The extent of Gibson's exasperation showed in his dusty eyes, steeling to a deeper grey. "You allow yourself to be a dupe in Tim's abuse. Do you honestly want to be complicit in a murder?"

"No, no. I'm not involved in any murder." Nick choked back his fears. He was quivering visibly now, his seat squeaking with the vibration. "It's just that Robbie drove Tim nuts with his skimpy pants and wiggling his butt. It's got nothing to do with me."

Scottie leaned forward about to confront Nick about the feud with Robbie. Possibly a lover's feud. Gibson laid his hand on her arm realizing what she was going to say. He preferred to keep the quarrel under wraps for now. They had no confirmation—just David's perception.

Nick sat alone on the bleachers as the detectives made their way out of the cold arena. The anguish in his eyes looked real as he was likely sensing he was a suspect.

"A print on a box is pretty useless for an arrest. We need prints on the condom wrap. Damn." Gibson thought Nick would break if they confronted him. He had pushed as hard as he could. No such luck. Nick was scared, but he wasn't going to confess to anything.

They made their way through the mucky grass.

"Tim is in the thick of it. I just know it," Gibson said.

Scottie had become silent, neither agreeing nor disagreeing. She drove them into town to meet with Jason's wife. On the way, Gibson phoned David's spouse to confirm his alibi. He thought a phone call would suffice for the time being.

"Hello." Jackie answered on the third ring.

Gibson spoke for a few minutes. She corroborated that David had gone to work at six thirty. He thanked her and said he would get in contact if he needed anything else.

"Why the shortcut?" Scottie asked. She was stunned that Gibson didn't want a personal interview.

"David discovered the body. Not a wise move for a killer to make. He seems like a smart guy. We have his alibi for now anyway."

"Yeah. I can appreciate that."

Scottie found a spot on Broughton—not easy to find parking downtown—and they wandered over to Wharf Street for a natter with Tammy. Her work was next door to the Old Victoria Custom House. As they passed the building, Gibson noted it was designated a national historic site in the 1980s. He stopped to marvel at the three-storey red brick structure with its mansard roof. Its prime waterfront location overlooked the city harbour.

They walked on and entered the foyer of Tammy's office and looked for the directory. Victoria Real Estate was on the second floor. They took the stairs climbing two steps at a time to arrive at a wide corridor. All the organizations had glass fronts so the detectives could see inside to the reception areas of each business. As they paraded past, they saw workers tapping on laptops, clinging to phones and huddled in groups. Most likely gossiping. At the furthest office, Tammy was perched on a stool at the front counter. At the party she had worn a tall conical hat with shaggy black hair poking out. Her hair tied into a ponytail now was not much tidier. The smirk on her face with the corners of her mouth frozen upward was about the same as well. Her wrinkled flowered blouse was tucked into a creased brown skirt. She was frumpy looking for an agency environment.

They presented themselves and accompanied her down a rear hallway, her hips swaying as she trotted to her destination. Tammy gestured to a cramped conference chamber with a huge oval table taking up the entire space. Cushy leather swivel chairs were negligently left where they had been shoved aside after the last meeting. As soon as they sat down Gibson got straight to the point.

"You live near the university by Gyro Park. When does Jason leave in the morning?"

"Same as me," she said. "Although you can see I have further to travel."

"What about on Monday? Was that any different?"

"Monday?" Tammy wavered as she thought it over. "Yeah. Our normal six fifteen." She chewed at a nail.

"Jason starts at seven," Gibson said. He raised his eyebrows in question.

"He stops for coffee," Tammy answered. A snarky intonation had crept into her voice. The pasted smile hinted at contempt.

"Where's that?"

"I suppose the Best Of Coffee around the corner from us." She shrugged, backing down her scorn just a smidgen. "Sometimes he goes to Ottiva across the street from there."

Gibson looked over at Scottie. They rose at the same time.

"Thanks, Tammy. You've been a tremendous help."

She gave an exaggerated pout, shifting the corners of her mouth down.

They bounded down the steps to Wharf Street. As they ambled down the lane to their vehicle Scottie said, "What a b…"

"Take it easy. Anyway we found out that Jason doesn't have an alibi unless someone at the café can vouch for him."

"Feel like a coffee?"

Chapter 21

Gibson fell back in his seat and closed his eyes. He was paying little attention to the radio until he caught one word. It made him bolt upright and bark out a curse.

"Damn. You've got to be kidding." He gazed open-mouthed at Scottie. "Snow. A snowfall warning."

They stopped at the station to swap vehicles. Half-way down the passage to the lower level, he received a call from forensics so he changed directions and headed to the lab. Scottie went to the basement garage to fetch his vehicle. The four-wheel drive would get them through the worst blizzard in a heartbeat. With the press of a button, the engine fired up with a roar. She loved the power of the V8 engine even if it was an ecoboost. The tires grabbed the concrete and climbed the ramp in three seconds.

The lab technician paced up and down the hall, kicking at the dust on the floor awaiting his fate. Gibson bounced off the last step and rounded the corner. A harried-looking Jocko stood still when he heard the rumbling off the stairs. His rumpled clothing hung from his thin frame, and his dull eyes hid the usual humorous intelligence. He darted toward the detective, apologizing for something.

"Sorry. I screwed up." His gaze boomeranged off the walls—the man was in a tizzy. "I lost a folder of prints." He clutched at Gibson's sleeve and then released it, stepping backward. "I discovered them this morning and ran them right away."

"What prints?"

"The building maintenance guys. They got misplaced." Jocko passed over a binder.

Gibson took a brief look and cracked a smile.

"Not a problem."

"Phew!" Jocko walked back to his lab, his stride buoyant and his heart lighter too. It was a rare occurrence for him to make such a mistake. He had felt foolish.

Gibson hurried outside and scoured the street. The F150 was almost a block away, white smoke spewing out the tailpipe. The frosty air had slipped down from the north. He bounded down the road and hopped into the hot truck. Scottie could tell the news was favourable by the ear-to-ear grin. She hung on to every word as he explained about the print fiasco.

"Let's go to Cafe Ottiva first."

"All right."

The F150 tracked the wet roads as if the day was dry and balmy. Scottie found a spot close by and squeezed into the parking place. They hustled down the sidewalk, already feeling the dampness crystallizing to ice under their boots. The windows were steamed up. The great rush of frigid air contacting the hot, moist atmosphere at the single pane glass formed droplets of water. Little puddles on the sill had grown more prominent as the day advanced. They stepped into the humidity of the café. AJ sat alone at an oval table in the corner, a steaming mug of coffee warming his hands. He peered up when the door chime announced someone's arrival. Scottie made a beeline to the breakfast counter. She strolled past AJ, pointing at him with her chin and a modest version of her Cheshire cat smile on her lips.

"Hi there. May we join you?" Gibson was already getting comfortable in a well-worn chair opposite him.

"Sure." AJ gave a half-hearted shrug, glanced over at Scottie and continued drinking his coffee.

With the sandwiches and lattes on order, she lingered at the counter and questioned the owner. Did he know Jason? From the maintenance shed. The supervisor. Was he a frequent customer? No. The owner recognized his regulars—Jason wasn't one of them. The owner's wife stirred beside him, nodding in agreement. Scottie moved to the table and grabbed a chair next to AJ.

"We were hoping to catch up with you," Gibson said.

"Oh," AJ replied. His muscles went rigid.

"So the crew was at the safety meeting, I understand. Anyone pop out? To the washroom? Grab a cigarette?"

"Maybe." AJ scratched the back of his neck and snorted an uneasy laugh. He cast down his eyes.

"What about you?" Gibson studied him.

"Well, I took off for a smoke."

"When?"

"Five-fifty. Or thereabouts." He pulled at his lips.

Scottie made notations in her journal as AJ spoke.

"See anybody?"

"A homeless guy was rooting through the garbage bin. That happens most mornings."

"What's his name?"

He lifted his shoulders.

"What was he wearing?"

"Homeless clothes, I guess." AJ stopped, realizing what he had just said. So derogatory. "His boots looked new, come to think of it."

"Did you see his face?"

"No. He had on a hoodie."

Gibson let that info drift into the 'may be important later' file. He had something significant that needed to be cleared up.

"Did you notice anything else while you were hanging around outside?" A sardonic grin flitted across Gibson's mouth. "Did you do anything besides have a puff, AJ?" He stared at him with narrowed eyes.

AJ swallowed, the lump prominent as it rolled down. He peered down at his boots. When he looked up, Gibson was scowling.

"There was a bat."

Gibson shot a candid glimpse at Scottie, then shifted back to AJ.

"And?"

"I picked it up. That's all."

"Why didn't you report this before?" Gibson demanded.

"Nobody asked. It slipped my mind. How would I know you cared?" Spots of colour appeared on his cheeks.

"That explains your prints." Gibson raised his eyebrows, thinking that was three different reasons.

"I just told you I picked the bat up. I didn't kill the guy. Jeez." AJ jerked back in his seat.

Gibson tried to rattle him more.

"Did Tony step out of the meeting at all?"

"I don't know. I couldn't see him."

"Tony wasn't in charge?" Gibson asked in disbelief. He shifted in his seat.

"No. Keith. You know, the assistant supervisor."

Gibson turned toward Scottie. Did someone in the meeting commit the crime? He opened his mouth but didn't speak. No. It was an outside chance only. He didn't think there would have been enough time. But they could have seen something. He studied AJ's bruised face.

"What happened to you?" He pointed at the blue creeping out from under the bandage.

"Nothing."

Gibson steeled his grey gaze.

"I got hit over the head."

"What? You got into a fight?"

"No. I got hit on the head from behind. Coming back to the shop. I went out for a smoke."

"Somebody ambushed you?"

"Yeah." He touched the plaster on his cheek.

"Why didn't you tell us earlier?" Gibson threw up his hands.

The welder just pulled his usual shrug.

"Any idea why someone would do that? Did you see something?"

"Not that I know." AJ twisted his mouth sideways.

Gibson shot another quick glance at Scottie. She was clicking her fingers against the tabletop.

"Anything else you would like to add?" Gibson was in a bad mood now with things going on and nobody talking. His thoughts wandered over the possibilities. Was it the murderer who had tried to harm AJ? Why? Was AJ unwittingly a witness? Maybe the homeless guy wasn't a homeless guy but the killer. It seemed likely that AJ had seen something he either forgot or thought meant nothing. Or he didn't want to tell. His mind spun.

He was about to ask another question when AJ dropped a bomb—someone's dirty little secret.

"Did you know Tim is Tony's nephew?"

"That's interesting," Gibson said. His thoughts were racing again. If Tony did step outside for something...Did Tony smoke? Did he see somebody? Tim? That would be sweet.

AJ looked around the room and remained quiet. He was somewhat flustered.

"If you think of anything else, call me," Gibson said. He pulled out a card and handed it to AJ. "Anything, whether it seems important or not."

AJ took it and shoved it into his shirt pocket.

Gibson thrust his chair aside and headed out. Scottie followed suit. The wind howled around the building and hooked the door as he pulled it open. It crashed into the wall twice before he could secure the catch. They dropped their heads against the squall and sprinted to the truck.

"Well, he sure had us running in circles," Scottie said. "Do you think there is a connection?"

"There is." Gibson barked back, his temper getting the better of him.

Scottie buttoned up.

"Why don't you go over to Best Of Coffee?" Gibson offered, toning down his rhetoric.

"I've had ample coffee thanks."

"Find out if Jason was there on Monday. I'm going over to have a chat with Andrew."

Scottie looked at him but didn't challenge his motives. She leaped out and grabbed her coat from the rear cab.

"Meet you at the shed in an hour."

* * *

Gibson took the main drag to the university. As he passed the arena, he glanced over to the marquee and let out a small yelp. Two men were standing rather close. He first recognized Nick who was shuffling his feet in the dirt and nodding his head. His brother-in-law was leaning on the wall, talking a mile a minute. Not a care in the world.

Gibson sped up. He parked his truck next to a Mustang, hauled out his cell and stabbed at the speed dial button assigned to Andrew. On the third ring he answered.

"Hi. Are you in your office?" Gibson asked. "I'm in the parking lot at the university."

There was a lengthy silence. "I'm on my way," he finally said, his voice squeaky. He disconnected the call.

Gibson lowered the phone slowly, struggling to figure out how to approach this problem. He put the cell in his upper jacket pocket and remained still for a few minutes, drumming his fingers on the steering wheel. He got out and looked at the thickening cloud cover. It seemed winter was on its way. He took the elevator to the top floor and strode down the light mustard-coloured corridor to the office.

Andrew was unwinding in his leather armchair. He appeared breathless from the dash across the campus and up the several sets of stairs. He pointed to a lone seat in front of his desk. Gibson sat down on a straight-backed chair.

"Don't want students to hang around too long." Andrew chuckled.

Gibson issued a noise of acknowledgement and unzipped his jacket. The room was overheated or he was. Because of what he had to do next? He wasn't sure. In the end he decided to be forthright.

"Is Nick more than an acquaintance?"

"You saw us." Not a question, more a fact spoken out loud. Andrew shrunk into the seat. His gaunt face was the same colour as the hallway, a sickly yellow. He clasped and unclasped his hands as if he needed consoling. Finally, he grabbed a hold of his courage and looked at Gibson, a rigid grimace overtaking his mouth.

Gibson nodded.

"You'll want to know everything," Andrew said.

"Are you all right?" Gibson's eyes showed a concern that had no strings attached.

Andrew stared at the window. The glass was dappled with bright spots left behind by the rain. He pressed one hand over his lips to hold back a cry. He began with agonizing slowness, letting out a groan from behind his palm.

"I'm gay." He spit it out.

Gibson was momentarily stunned into silence. This was a secret that could lead to humiliation or worse, persecution by his fellow workers. Not for him to judge. He tried to make eye contact, but Andrew twisted his vision to the floor.

"Nick and I started out as friends and then…" He pushed away from the desk and hit his knee. "Damn. I should have mentioned my involvement. What was I thinking?"

Andrew placed his hands into prayer under his chin and slumped his head. His world had gone black.

"With staff. Oh my god. What have I done?" Andrew knew that everything that he had worked for could lie in ruins. His eyes dampened with regret. And maybe fear for his future.

"It's okay." Gibson almost regretted confronting him. This tryst probably didn't have anything to do with his investigation. And even if it did, could he take the next step? It was something that he wasn't willing to think about now.

"You're not alone."

Andrew looked up with hope in his eyes.

"I read your blog about shattered people. I understand your pain. When I was a kid. When my brother died." His grey eyes clouded with a mist from behind. "I wasn't there for him." Gibson lost his thought in time. He barely heard the ring. The buzzing in his ears had grown into a crescendo. His cell vibrated in his pocket. He yanked it out.

"Gibson."

Andrew heard shouting from the other side.

"A jacket? Be right there." He rose unexpectedly, knocking his chair over in confusion. A flush travelled from his neck to his cheeks.

"I have to go."

Chapter 22

Scottie had walked over to Best Of Coffee. It was a busy café, much more so than the Ottiva. That meant more staff, more schedule changes to sort through and less personal interaction with the customers. There was an array of tables, chairs and booths scattered throughout the room. A rough wooden shelf at the front window had tall stools lined up along its length to take up the slack in the peak hours. For the amount of people in the place at the moment, being between coffee breaks, it seemed peak hour was the norm. There was a lot of action going on—students texting and snapchatting, geeks in the corner tapping on their laptops and moms dragging youngsters away from fingering the floor displays. The line to the cashier was daunting, a hotchpotch of bodies swaying and rocking. It started at the cash registers, passed the glass food cooler and stretched to the door with several individuals standing outside.

Scottie scanned the people behind the high counter. Who was rushing around the most? Who looked in charge at a rate of pay just pennies above the rest of the team? A dark-haired girl in her thirties stood out. She was darting from one workstation to the next, barking out requests, tidying up spills and looking completely frazzled. It took mere seconds for Scottie to capture her attention with a quick wave in her direction. The girl would always be on the alert for any warning sign of trouble. Nip it in the bud.

"Could I have a word with you?" Scottie flashed her badge.

"Sure," the girl said. She unconsciously bit the side of her lip in consternation. "Is there an issue?"

"No. Just need to ask a few questions," Scottie assured her, giving a moderate version of her famous grin.

The girl motioned Scottie behind the counter through the staff door to a little lunchroom. She plunked down on a rickety steel folding chair, perching so near to the edge of the seat it almost collapsed beneath her.

Scottie sat opposite, wary of her weight on the flimsy seat.

"Do you know Jason from UVic, the maintenance foreman?"

"He comes in here a lot." She released a pent-up breath, relief overcoming her features. Okay, nothing to do with the café or her job.

"Was he here this past Monday morning?" Scottie asked, pleased that the girl had recognized Jason by name.

"Possibly. I was working that day. But each day merges into another though." She plucked a pencil from a jar and tapped it on edge.

"Can you think about it? Anything unusual about that morning that would give you a clearer picture." Scottie scrutinized the oval face as she waited for her to consider the not so remote past.

The girl glanced at the clock hanging above the microwave, rocking in the chair as she thought about it. She tossed the pencil on the table.

"Sorry. What's this about?" she asked. Then, abruptly, she brought her palms to her mouth and exclaimed, "Oh. It's about the murder." Her eyes misted up as she stared at Scottie and murmured, "Is Jason okay?" She stopped. A perplexed expression came over her face. "Is he involved?"

"No. No. Just routine." Scottie evaded the question but realized the papers had picked up the story but not the victim's identity. "Could you find out who else worked that morning? See if anyone remembers serving Jason." Scottie handed over her card and pushed the chair backward.

"Sure," the girl said as she placed the card into her apron pocket. She jumped to her feet, wrenching her ankle and collapsed against the table. Scottie grabbed her arm to cut short her fall. A blush seared through her freckled skin. She recovered and retreated, keeping her eyes averted. Scottie followed her to the front and flipped a little wave as she swung to the exit. The girl gazed at the door long after she had disappeared.

Scottie headed back to the maintenance shed. She wanted answers from Tony. No more fooling around. What was really going on during that meeting? Not so cut and dry. People wandering in and out. If she had to pry it out of him… She was particularly looking forward to spilling the beans about her knowledge of him and Tim. It was a delicious thought. When did she get so vindictive? She sighed deeply and carried on. As Scottie walked by the garage doors, she saw Jason bolt to the stairwell. Was the foreman avoiding her? Probably. But she was looking for the supervisor so she strode across the graveled yard to the workshop. She snatched the handle just as Tony was stepping outside. Scottie tripped back to avoid running him over. Her immense mass towered over his fat, unkempt physique. A clash would have stung. The supervisor braked sharply and flung his fists up.

"Watch it."

"Tim's your nephew." The words rushed from her mouth before she could stop herself. Her fuse simmered and fizzled like a firecracker. She bit her tongue and winced at her unprofessional manner. Then she flashed the Cheshire grin in atonement.

"So what!" Tony retorted, his hackles standing on end.

Besides hiring your relations, nothing, thought Scottie. Then changing subjects, a modicum of geniality sweetening her approach.

"Well, we've learned that your safety meeting was…shall we say slack." Getting no reaction, she continued, "People coming and going as they pleased." She said it with honey on her tongue although the loathsome fat swine made her seethe.

"No idea what you're talking about," he said. Spit spewed from his mouth.

"Sure you do. We know that AJ left for a puff." She barked it out. That didn't last long. Back to vinegar.

"AJ was hardly gone a minute." Tony gnawed the inside of his cheek, the taste of blood filling his mouth. His gaze flicked to the other building.

"Oh. So you noticed and didn't tell us?" Scottie asked. "Besides, you weren't even in charge of the meeting. Maybe you skipped out."

A protracted silence followed before Tony spoke, fire in his eyes and on his tongue. "I didn't leave." He scratched the bald spot looking for the hair that had taken flight years ago. "Nobody else did either."

Scottie felt the vibration emanating from Tony's shaking limbs.

"Any washroom breaks?"

"No." Tony turned brusquely and raced across the courtyard. "You got it wrong," he shouted over his shoulder. He swung the door open and escaped up the stairs.

Scottie groaned and kneaded her forehead, trying to forestall a headache pulsating at her temple. She had meant to ask about AJ getting hit over the head.

A hammering sound coming from the workshop brought her back to the present. She was surprised when she entered the building to see the welder bent over at the farthest workbench. He must have slipped in by the rear door while she was pre-occupied with the supervisor. Was the door left unlocked? Did he have a key? Did everybody have access? Scottie moved in closer and watched as AJ beat the red-hot surface of the bracket, willing it into shape.

Patiently she stuck around for a gap in the clanging, to catch his attention. As she remained planted in one spot, her mind whirled with unanswered questions. She plucked out the journal to jot down reminders. The maintenance trucks. Who drove them after hours? What else? She tapped her pen on the book thinking of other issues. She glanced around the workshop, biding her time and feeling brain dead. A frigid gust of wind from an open window sent a paper bag scurrying by. She followed the abandoned brown sack as it tumbled across the cold cement floor. It hit the wall and stopped below the line of mostly empty hooks.

A shiny moss-green puffy parka caught her eye sitting all alone on the last rung. She stared at a spray of miniature spots that dotted the front of the jacket. A perplexed look washed over her face until what she saw kicked into her rational mind. This wasn't dirt. Her instincts told her it was something more. She yanked out latex gloves from her pocket and slapped them on. A whiff of copper struck her nostrils as she fingered the parka—the scent of blood. She couldn't know if it was from an injured finger or spatter from the murder weapon. She tugged on the collar. On the inside, faded initials were marked with a black Sharpie, TRS.

"Where did this come from?" she demanded.

"I don't know." AJ swung from his bench to face her.

"Whose initials are these?" She pointed at the letters. Anticipation sent a nervous kind of energy tingling through her to her fingertips.

He gave a half-hearted shrug and shoved his hands in his pockets.

Scottie placed the jacket back in its place, tore off her gloves and fumbled in her pocket for her phone. Two calls—forensics to dispatch a crime scene technician promptly, and the inspector.

As Gibson rode over to the maintenance yard, he was thinking about something else. Who was the blurred person in the Facebook picture? He would have to examine the photo again—with a magnifying glass. Looking up, he saw the clouds piling into a sinister mass. His eyebrows converged into a singular clump. The creases on his forehead would become permanent soon. There were so many unanswered questions. He squeezed his fists on the steering wheel tighter. He pulled his F150 by the garage doors next to a white Chevy with grey lettering on the door. He wondered if Scottie had questioned the dog walker about the truck yet. He added that to his mental list of things to find out. They were all working overtime. All his team were pursuing leads, sorting what might be relevant and what was insignificant. They were painstakingly hunting for any evidence—a direction. This jacket could prove to be the turning point.

A van pulled onto the gravel and parked next to him. It was a crime scene guy, Raymond Dolinski, transferred in from Alberta. They stepped out of their vehicles in unison. The technician's outfit was neat and clean which was a tough thing to manage in his line of work. He looked stern with a curled upper lip and flared nostrils, but his eyes crinkled at the corners in a smile. He saluted his superior with a snappy flick of his hand. Gibson gestured back with a beam of acknowledgement. People assumed Raymond was a prickly individual because of his exterior appearance, but he wasn't.

They entered the shop together, one man trailing behind the other. Scottie was seated on a stool with her cell stuck onto her ear. She bobbed her head several times and muttered a few words before she hung up. She pointed to the rear wall where the bloodied jacket stood in plain sight and unpretentious.

"Could you make this a top priority, Raymond?" Gibson asked.

"You bet." He plucked a huge evidence bag out of the case he was carrying and shoved the parka inside, labeling the outside with a black Sharpie. "Okay. I'll be on my way." He slipped out. They could hear the pinging of stones hitting the metal sheathing as he sped off.

"Down to earth guy," Gibson said.

"I think Jason and Tony are in the upstairs office."

They crossed the courtyard and flew up the now familiar stairs. Behind the closed door, a heated discussion drifted into the hallway. Scottie knocked loudly to get a reaction. The entrance swung open with Tony still holding the handle. He stretched over, balancing on the edge of his seat almost to the point of toppling. With some effort, he corrected himself and drove his chair into the floor with a smack. He bared his teeth. Jason was seated sideways at his desk with his feet spread out in front and hands behind his neck. He had a haughty sneer that formed hollows in his cheeks. When he saw who his visitors were, his lips tightened. With a flick of his hand, he pointed to the low bench under the notice board. Gibson dropped onto the hard surface, wishing he had stayed standing. He sat uncomfortably with his knees touching his chest. Scottie stood by the exit, arms held at her side. The room was cramped with four bodies. Tony made a move to leave, but Gibson waved him back.

"Need a word with both of you. We found a bloodied jacket. Any guesses whose it is?"

Tony and Jason exchanged a fleeting glance but remained silent.

"There's an insignia on the shoulder with one hundred and fifty under a Canadian flag," Scottie spoke up. "Does that help?"

Tony was gazing in all directions. To the bulletin board, the mounted diplomas and the ceiling fan. He made no eye contact and bit at his nails.

"That was a special order for the Confederation anniversary. We all got one," Jason said.

"What about you? The jacket was in your shop?" He fixed his stare on Tony's double chin.

Tony raised his palms in a 'don't know' gesture and returned to examining his nails.

"A few got worn out. Some guys took them home," Jason said, trying to be accommodating.

"What about the initials inside the collar?"

"What are they?"

"TRS."

A trickle of sweat rolled down Tony's temple and gathered at his chin. He pulled a tissue from a hidden pocket in his shoddy sweatpants and wiped his face. He stole a glance toward Jason. For a moment they locked eyes.

Gibson noticed the mute communication but didn't understand what it meant so he guessed, "Tim Sanderson?"

"I suppose." Jason brushed a fleck of imaginary dirt from his neck.

"Anyone else with those initials?" Gibson let the crew names flash by his vision. He came up with another name.

"Tony Sarcone."

Tony folded his arms over his stocky trunk. "I don't have a middle name. No R. And it's Anthony." He barked out a laugh. The room resounded with the heavy bellow.

"What's Tim's middle name?"

Tony snubbed him.

"Don't know," Jason said. His half grimace contorted his features.

"Where is Tim working?"

"He wasn't feeling well and left early."

"Okay." Gibson cast a look over to his partner.

"What do you know about AJ getting hit over the head?"

"What? Where?" Jason sat up.

"He got taken by surprise in the workshop."

Both men were rendered speechless and folded into their chairs.

"Any ideas who would do that?"

"Is he okay?" Jason asked. "He should have reported it."

"We're looking into it. We'll talk again. Let's go, Scottie."

Gibson battled to get off the bench and almost stumbled when his leg cramped. They trotted down the steps and hopped into the truck.

"Where are we going?" Scottie asked.

"Tim's place."

* * *

Scottie fired up the truck and roared down the street to Brentwood Bay. She manoeuvred through the light traffic and reached Hagan Road in record time. They parked on the grass verge because there weren't any curbs in this part of town. The house they were looking for was one house up from the corner. It was a nineteen fifties post-war structure with the typical white clapboard siding and black asphalt shingle roofing. The window trim was a deep shade of purple. There were no lights on and the drapes were drawn. No one answered the door when Scottie knocked. She tried again, banging louder with her fist. Nobody was home.

"I thought he went home sick." Gibson lingered on the porch. He was sure this was a hate crime and Tim was the killer. He wasn't willing to leave in a hurry. Maybe the guy just popped up the street to a store.

Scottie could tell that Gibson was digging in about the hate crime hypothesis. She was doubtful the jacket proved anything. But she wasn't the boss.

"A homeless guy could have taken it from the garbage bin," Scottie said. She couldn't stop herself from speaking up—never was a wallflower.

"It looks brand new. Who would throw it out?"

"Could have been scooped at the party?" Scottie suggested.

"Then what? Returned it? And why? That sounds absurd."

"They don't lock doors around there. People are in and out of that place like characters in a movie."

The wrangling went on. Who had access to the coat? Why did it show up now? Why not fling it away—far away?

"Here's a theory that meets all the criteria," Gibson said. He wasn't giving up his bully assumption to something else that easily.

Scottie scrunched her face into a 'here it comes.'

"Tim was trying to get rid of the jacket. He thought nobody was around and was going to throw it in the back bin, but AJ walked in on him. So he whacks him over the head, puts the jacket on the closest hook and splits. How's that?" He grinned at her.

Scottie didn't see it that way so she said nothing. After ten minutes of standing around, there was still no sign of Tim. Gibson fumbled in his pocket for his cell, his fingers turning numb.

"Jocko. Anything further? We're at Tim's house."

"No. Scottie phoned me not that long ago. Nothing has changed."

Jocko sounded perturbed.

"But don't worry. I'll stay until I get the test results. I'll call you," he said somewhat abashed, remembering that Gibson had let him off the hook about the misplaced prints.

"Okay, thanks." Gibson glanced at his watch. He had lost all sense of time. He shivered from the bitter cold, the bite of the wind forming small bumps on his arms.

"We can't stay here all night," Scottie said. The cold reached into her bones.

Chapter 23

The snow was falling heavily soon after Gibson dropped Scottie at the station. He advanced through the city streets, exited the freeway and manoeuvred through the side lanes. Five inches had accumulated and stuck to the surface, unwilling to melt. Visibility reduced by the driving sleet made him bend forwards into the windshield. There were no snowplows anywhere in sight. As the silver dust drifted around his slow-moving vehicle, he felt shrouded by an aura of solitude. Few cars shared the road with him, more were abandoned in awkward angles along the curb. No people, no footsteps or paw tracks were imprinted in the powder that collected on the sidewalks. He turned off Verdier Avenue for the last stretch to home, his beacon of light barely discernible. It was a curious sense of disquietude he seldom experienced. Is this how Katherine must suffer? Cut off from people. Emotions deadened by blank despondency?

Gibson pulled into the driveway, shut off the ignition and let the tension sweep aside. He wasn't certain if his melancholy thoughts or the daunting ride home had stiffened his muscles. Maybe he was turning into an authentic local, giving in to the nerve-racking ordeal of driving in the snow. He chuckled to himself and patted the hood, grateful for the four-wheel-drive vehicle.

Katherine had taken vigilance by the window. Like a falcon eyeing mice as they scuttled through the grass, she stared into the dense flurries watching for signs of her husband. From the top of the lane, dim headlights appeared. She watched as the truck wavered down the icy track toward their house and crunched to a halt in the driveway.

Gibson made a speedy dash to the door. He yanked it open and stepped into the heat with great white flakes chasing behind. She shivered as the icy wind blew right through her sweater. He thought her trembling body came from a coldness inside her, not from the arctic air that had blasted in.

Katherine clenched and unclenched her hands. She found social affairs difficult, and today the snow was adding an extra element to her uneasiness. This would be Heather's first art display at the famous South Side Studio. The gallery hosted showings of upcoming Canadian artists, making this a significant solo exhibition. It was a big step up for Heather. Victoria had a vibrant artist community, and the competition was fierce. They could not miss it.

"The show is hours away. They'll have the roads plowed by then," Gibson said.

He nudged her playfully down the hallway and into the kitchen. The scents of peppery oregano, citrus and marjoram filled the air. Lasagne. He couldn't think of a better way to warm the soul on a frosty evening along with a glass of red wine, of course. While they were eating, he heard the plow go by. It rattled the windows as it rumbled down the lane. He checked out the front window. The steel blade had left a glaze on the road surface, but it had stopped snowing. He headed to the bedroom to get ready. He put on a plain white shirt with tailored black slacks. A black wool sweater almost hid his silver and black tie.

"I'm going to warm up the truck." Gibson donned his coat and woolen scarf and marched outside into the frigid night. The clouds had thickened and a brisk wind brought a chill to the air. He exhaled a puff of white fog and hopped into the cab. He fiddled with the knobs to adjust the heat and waited. Katherine opened the door and a beam of light crossed over the frozen lawn. She wrapped her arms around her body, hesitated fleetingly and dashed to the truck.

Gibson backed out onto the street. The tires gripped the road surface better than he thought they would. He peered sideways at Katherine. She sat rigidly with a seat belt snuggled across her chest holding her upright. All roads into Victoria were clear and the traffic was light. Snow had dusted the town and turned it into a magical land. Conifer branches from the majestic fir trees were bent low with the extra white weight. Their needles brushed the ground and left scratch marks on the thick blanket. Rooftops stacked six inches deep made the buildings look like gingerbread houses. Several humps on the roadside disguised vehicles covered in the plow wash. He turned right off Blandshard to View. There were plenty of parking spots, few people being out and about. He had hoped the snowstorm wouldn't deter the art patrons.

Gibson whipped around to the passenger side and released the door. Katherine held onto the dashboard for just an instant before she swung her legs round. He had worn plain sensible leather boots, not as trendy as her high heeled ones. The roads had been plowed and sanded but not the sidewalks. Katherine took baby steps on the slickened surfaces. He held her in tight for safety—and comfort. Fine lines creased the corner of her eyes, and her lips squeezed into a pout. As they got closer to the gallery, music blared out to the pavement to welcome the guests. At the entrance, a cloakroom attendant hung their coats and handed him a ticket stub for retrieval. Next, a youthful girl dressed all in black approached them with a tray of bubbly wine. They grabbed a glass and advanced farther into the hubbub.

The studio was an impressive room with a twelve-foot flat ebony ceiling. LED track lighting beamed down onto the floor and quelled the harsh shadows. The walls were painted a stormy gray and reflected the light with a soft glow, making the artwork come alive. The wide-open space invited a spirit of analysis and exploration.

Gibson kept Katherine close to his side while they ambled through the studio. The watercolours were subtle in their hues and tones—so unlike the artist. Each art piece was a glimpse into Heather's mind. Bodies pressed into them with everyone moving in different directions. They wandered. They jostled. And shuffled on from one painting to another. He steered them through the throng toward the grinning artist.

The noise level was high with voices bouncing off the soaring ceilings. Above the chatter, Gibson heard a discordant voice at the far end of the room. He glimpsed over and saw Jason and his wife in a heated exchange. Suddenly becoming aware of unwanted attention, Tammy stalked away. Jason spotted Gibson and headed over.

Gibson's cell vibrated in his pocket. He answered it straight away. The din of voices echoing in the room made it hard to hear. He pressed the cell into his ear and leaned into the earpiece. His eyes flashed as he listened. He hung up and punched in a number.

"I'll make it brief."

Katherine smiled.

He felt a presence behind him and turned to catch Jason hovering close by. A shift to the right and he was out of earshot. Scottie answered on the second ring.

"Jocko just called. It's Robbie's blood on the jacket," Gibson said. "It all points to Tim. The prints on the bat. He has no alibi. The jacket with his initials. He's a homophobe."

"We don't know that it's Tim's jacket. You're pushing the envelope." Scottie didn't want to jump to conclusions. Gibson did.

"It's him," he cried out and quickly covered his mouth with his hand. He glanced around, but nobody had noticed his outburst.

"Look. We don't have enough evidence for an arrest even if the jacket is Tim's."

"You're right. Something else Jocko told me that's interesting." He gave her the scoop.

"Wow, really. Talk to you tomorrow." She disconnected.

"Let's go." Katherine had managed to remain calm for the evening. She had actually enjoyed herself, but there was a limit to her ability to mingle.

"Okay, sweetie." Gibson fumbled in his pocket for the cloakroom ticket. Before he could make a move, Jason marched over and blocked their forward progress.

"Was that about the case?" he asked.

"No. Not at all," Gibson lied. He thought this guy was so hot and cold. Now he understood what the workers meant. Yelling at them one minute and wanting to bike with them the next. He was nosy too.

"I wanted to invite you and your wife to a small memorial for Robbie. It's Saturday morning at the yard." His smile fell lifeless.

"Thanks for the invite. We'll try to make it. I forget how tough it is on the employees when something like this happens." He grinned and forced himself past Jason to get their coats. Katherine was hanging onto his arm. No way was he going to that. He always kept his work life separate from his private life, although he couldn't disconnect his thoughts from each reality. They buttoned up their coats and wound scarves around their collars to ward off the cold that they knew would hit them. Right on schedule, a burst of snowflakes blasted their faces as they stepped outside. Katherine covered her face from the heavy deluge of twirling crystals driven down from a pure white sky. The fresh layer of snow crunched as they hurried down the street. Gibson lowered his face against the biting wind. The swirling icy fingers blinded him, and he almost didn't see the truck a few spots ahead of his own vehicle. It was a university truck. He guessed it must be Jason driving it because nobody else from the yard was at the gala. Not that he noticed anyway. That brought a ton of unanswered questions to his mind again. But it was about the jacket now. He would visit Tim first thing tomorrow—early, really early.

Chapter 24

The flurries had fallen steadily during the night, blanketing everything in sight. It was six in the morning, but reflection off the snow provided an artificial brightness. Katherine was sleeping so Gibson slipped out of the house to carry out his mission. He planned to surprise Tim with a wake-up call.

It was tough going for a bit on the slippery roads. The overnight temperature had dropped below freezing and left large patches of black ice here and there. But he managed to manoeuvre the truck up Verdier Avenue, plowing through the drifts without getting stuck. He turned right on Hagan and crawled slowly down Clarke Road to his destination. Most households had darkened windows as he progressed down the street. People were still burrowed under their eiderdowns—it would take coffee brewing to dig them out.

This time, as he approached Tim's home, he saw a glow of light behind the curtains. The white painted dwelling with snow-laden roof had all but faded into the wintery scenery. An illumination in the backyard suggested someone had let the dog out for a pee. Gibson didn't actually know if Tim had a dog. He pulled into the driveway and headed for the front door. After knocking twice with no answer, he wandered down the side of the house toward the back. The pavement was shoveled but still quite slick like the roads. He heard a buzzing noise coming from the rear, so he kept on going. As Gibson rounded the final corner, Tim twisted toward the trespasser. A flash glinted off the axe dangling by his leg.

The detective stopped dead in his tracks holding both hands up at shoulder height. A hearty laugh erupted from the bushes to his right. Tim relaxed his stance and chuckled along with the neighbour hidden from his view. He looked over to where the offending guffaw had resounded. In the next yard, he saw a man leaning on the ramshackle fence. The shadow of a lofty evergreen tree cloaked his face. He was dressed in jeans, a lumberjack shirt and goose-filled vest. His hair stuck out from under a toque. The man gave a shortened wave. A large whack sounded to his left. Gibson turned his gaze back to Tim who had struck the axe into a nearby chopping block.

Tim removed his leather gloves and tossed them aside. He snorted and wiped his nose with the tail of his shirt. Gibson realized the guy had been splitting wood. He took a cursory glance around the lot. There were several rounds of cedar, an assortment of axes and a chainsaw with a UVic label glued on the side. Closer to the house under the eaves was a heap of kindling with a jacket strewn on top.

"What the hell are you doing here?" Tim snarled.

"Is that yours?" Gibson said, paying no heed to the hostility. He went to the wood pile and picked up the coat. He held it up to the light so he could read the inside collar. It was marked 'Tim Sanderson' in block letters.

Tim glared at him.

"This must be yours. What about the saw?" He pointed at a brand new saw with its label declaring UVic the owner.

Tim shoved his hands into his pockets and gave an indifferent shrug.

"Good idea. Don't want it stolen." Gibson pointed at the collar and tossed the jacket back on the woodpile. He thought Tim was such an ass.

"What do you want?"

"Do you know anybody with the initials, TRS?"

"Sure."

"Who?"

"Trent Robert Spencer," he said. "Robert for Robbie."

Gibson was stunned. It was Robbie's coat covered in blood. That didn't make any sense.

"You haven't explained why you're here," Tim said. "Why are you so obsessed with my jacket?"

"You don't have an alibi for Monday." Gibson didn't owe him any answers.

"I do." A wry smirk twisted his mouth.

"Excuse me." The neighbour cleared his throat.

"Do you know something?" Gibson looked over to the man.

"Are you talking about this past Monday?"

"Yes."

"Well, Tim was just telling me about the murder and that he didn't have an alibi." He rubbed his gloved hands together to keep them warm. Gibson braced himself.

"Funny thing is that on Monday morning I was staring out my window at the side there." He stopped to point to the window facing Tim's backyard. "I was waiting for a taxi to take me to the airport. I saw Tim chopping wood."

"What time?" Gibson grumbled.

"The cab was late. So about six thirty. I almost missed my flight."

Tim strutted over to the fence, and the men gave a high-five pump. Tim puffed out his chest. Gibson scowled at him.

"Why didn't you say something before?"

"I just found out myself. My neighbour got back from his trip last night." The smirk stayed.

Gibson had seldom felt so deflated. He thanked the man, took a hard look at Tim and left. As he stomped out of the yard, puffs of steam blew from his mouth. He jumped into the F150 and fired it up. The clock read six so he headed downtown. The sun had broken free from the horizon and spilled its rays across his vision. He had been so involved in the conversation he hadn't noticed the sky had brightened to an azure blue, the intense blue of a cloudless fall day. It brought him no comfort. The blue only reflected his mood.

As he was driving down the freeway, he decided to skip the office and exited from the off-ramp to slip onto McKenzie Street. The route to the university had been cleared by plows, ready for the onslaught of pupils. He dropped into the Cafe Ottiva for a coffee and a cinnamon bun. From there, he pulled alongside the curb at the maintenance shed and remained in his truck drinking his latte and munching on a pastry. He thought about phoning Katherine, then chose not to disturb her. Today was the final exam—crucial but nerve-racking even for a composed individual. How would his wife handle it? He leaned back in his seat and relaxed against the rest. He would need to contact Scottie soon and give her the bad news. Tim was no longer a suspect. His hate crime theory had crashed. The bully was innocent. That was a laugh. He had been convinced the killer was Tim. They would have to start over. He picked up his cell to call Scottie, but it chirped. He glanced at the caller ID and moaned.

"Gibson."

"I haven't had an update for a while," the police chief said.

"We're working hard. Nothing yet, Chief." Gibson would have preferred to say they were getting close, but what did they have now? Zilch. So he faked it.

"I've asked Gunner to follow the money," he said and blew his nose.

"Don't turn this into a hate scandal."

Gibson remained silent so Rex added, "Do you hear me?"

"Yes, sir." It didn't matter anymore. A hate crime was off the table even for him.

The chief hung up.

Gibson got out of the truck and trudged through the snow to the maintenance building. No one was about. No one was in the garage. He trekked up the steep stairs. The lunchroom was empty. Jason's door was open, but he wasn't there. Should he wait or search for him in the shop? He couldn't remember if there were any trucks in the yard. He was stumbling around in a daze. He rested at the office door, trying to organize his plans. Two chairs were pushed toward the corner where the boots had been. He strode over to the bulletin board and flipped at the sheets pinned to the cork. Nothing much of importance here. There was a notice about dogs running loose, a sign-up sheet for overtime and a volunteer one for the approaching parade. He proceeded along the wall and studied the diplomas framed in black matte. Horticulture and business. Those made him think of Katherine. Gibson took out his cell to call. Still holding onto his phone, he plunged into the same chair he had occupied several days earlier when he had first done the interviews. He hesitated and dialed Scottie's number instead. It was time to admit his mistake. She answered on the first ring, evidently waiting for some word.

"Well. What happened this morning? Good or bad?"

"Bad." Better get to the point. Gibson filled her in on the details. The jacket, the initials, T R S, Robbie for Robert. Tim had an alibi collaborated by his neighbour. "And Rex called."

"What did he want? What did you tell him?"

"Not much. He wants the financial angle investigated more thoroughly. Which I presume means Jeff should be looked at more closely," Gibson said. Rex was right. What motive is there besides money?

"Revisit the entire crew," Scottie broke into Gibson's musings.

"Yeah. Maybe someone stole out of the meeting. Saw something or…?" Gibson swallowed the thickness in his throat. "What are you up to?"

"I'm working on the files. I might check out other campsites in the neighbourhood." She paused and added, "The homeless guy is on the table. Don't you think?"

"Maybe. Get the dog walker to look at the maintenance truck, too. Not sure why, but…" Gibson trailed off.

"Okay. I have the guy's name here." Scottie flipped through her notebook. "Liam."

She hung up.

Gibson rose from the chair and pocketed his phone. He would go to the shop. He bent over Jason's desk to inspect a photograph that he hadn't noticed before. It was Tammy dressed in a perky outfit on a sailboat. He heard footsteps and voices in the hallway. Jason and Tony strolled into the office. They were startled to see him.

"What are you doing? What do you want?" Tony demanded. His tone had a gruff edge to it. He pulled up a chair and plopped himself down.

Jason edged his way around the room and twisted into his chair. He pushed his hand over his chin.

"Why did you leave your former job, Tony?" Gibson asked. He stared at his bald spot and pudgy body. He was in rotten humour, he had to take it out on someone. The supervisor was the ideal guy.

"Better opportunity here. What's it to you?" he scoffed. His lips curled into a half smile; a half sneer.

"You were fired," Gibson said, meanness creeping into his speech. He didn't like either of these guys, and he was drained from their stonewalling him. "For sexual indiscretion," he underscored, narrowing his steely greys into a hard stare.

Tony slunk into his seat. The redness crept up his neck to his ears, eyes cast to the floor. He remained silent.

"The bloody jacket was found in your department. Anything to say for yourself?" Gibson was annoyed and wasn't holding back anymore.

Tony wiped his clammy palms on his sweatpants.

Gibson's phone rang, fortuitously interrupting him before he blew a gasket. It was Scottie.

"The girl at Best Of Coffee just called me."

He waited, holding his breath—it was becoming a habit.

"One of the employees saw Jason on Monday. He grabbed a coffee and quickly disappeared. Usually he sat by the window and drank his coffee."

Gibson forced the air out through his lips, making a rude sound.

"Okay. What time was that?"

"Somewhere around a quarter after six."

He studied Jason, with his grey hair and lifeless grey eyes, thanked Scottie and disconnected.

"A staff member at Best Of Coffee saw you on Monday," Gibson said. "You picked up a coffee and left."

Jason waved his hand in dismissal of the suggestion.

"I can't remember one day to the next if I stayed or not. How can a silly waitress be so certain?" he said. Disdain dripped through his remark.

Before Gibson could oppose that rationalization, his phone sounded again. As he listened, his face paled. He charged out the door.

Chapter 25

Katherine's panic attack had sent Gibson's optimism plummeting. After her frantic call, he dashed down the steps and out of the building. The sound of the slammed door reverberated in the stairwell. He galloped across the boulevard, ignoring the blare of a horn as he skipped on top of the snow bank onto the curb. Gibson sprinted through the rutted grass, spraying water as he jumped over large icy puddles. He yanked at the door and ran for the elevators. Ding. They were all in use. He whipped about and headed for the stairs. It was just one flight up, but he was drained by the time he entered the corridor. It was empty except for his wife.

Katherine was collapsed on the stone floor. Her legs pulled into her body, and arms wrapped securely around her shins, reminded Gibson of a pill bug curled into a ball. The flushed skin was clammy. Small drips of moisture under her nose glistened in the fluorescent light. Her breathing was stilted. Her wild eyes were riveted on the handbag and books strewn at her feet. She twitched at the approach of footsteps. Her lips, faded red, made a small heart when she opened her mouth.

"Oh, honey," she whimpered.

The overwrought intonation banged against his heart. Gibson slid down the wall onto the ground next to Katherine and leaned into his wife's aura. He stretched out a hand to stroke the ruddy cheek. It was burning hot. She drew her trembling limbs tighter into her body, making her sink deeper into the floor. He placed his arm around her shoulders and cradled her shivering body. Ten minutes passed. Fifteen. She scrunched her face, repressing tears that threatened to release down her cheeks, bringing black mascara with them. The vacant expression lightened as she firmed her jaw. He freed his hold when she tried to stand up.

"Not sure I can do this."

Katherine faltered at the door, gripping the jamb with slender fingers. Her slight frame looked taut from tension. A pause brought a slow trickle of sweat to her forehead. She mustered all her courage and stepped through the doorway. She glanced back, bounced on the balls of her feet and held her hands in prayer. The door was shut behind her.

* * *

It was done. Katherine had completed the exam and truly felt good about it. Now Gibson was free to enjoy his weekend, leaving Scottie in charge. Southwest winds had driven the clouds away and brought a balmy warmth. Snow from the early storm was melting fast—global warming. The shift in weather energized him. Equilibrium was restored. He skipped out the front door to the café with a weightlessness in his limbs. His buddy sat at the regular table by the window gazing over the light-dappled water. Waves gently striking the shore washed the rocks. Jesse didn't notice him until he plopped himself in the chair and snorted a throaty laugh.

"Hey. How's it going?" Jesse held up his hand to get Gibson a coffee, but the waitress was on it.

"Good."

Both remained taciturn, looking over the bay. Gibson knew he wouldn't be urged to talk about the current case. It was up to him to start any discussion.

"Doesn't look like a hate crime," Gibson said. He needed to shake off this setback. "My prime suspect got cleared yesterday."

He looked at Jesse. His smile was relaxed, but his eyes twinkled merrily. He grabbed this friendship. Recharged, fearless. "I was sure, but I was mistaken."

"No matter," was all Jesse countered. "Want someone to kayak with today?"

"Yeah, that would be great."

He could count on his buddy to cut to the chase. Let it go. The men finished their coffee and preceded down the ramp. They gathered their gear and slipped their boats into the ocean, setting off to the south arm of the inlet. Although the sun was pleasant on their faces, the breeze on the water kept them from feeling the heat. They would use the wind to their advantage and steal a little push down the waterway. As they swung out into Finlayson Arm waterway, Gibson looked up to the cell tower that marked the crest of the Malahat—a thousand feet above sea level—and the loftiest point of the highway leading through the hills to North Vancouver Island. As his gaze shifted to the east over the forested shoreline, the sunlight reflected off windows on the waterfront across the inlet.

Soon they were paddling smoothly in rhythm, side by side, listening to the chants of the wild. A gaggle of geese flew overhead, honking as they made their way to California. Jesse glanced over to Gibson and nodded his approval. For several hours they travelled along the shoreline undaunted by their screaming muscles. They halted for a snack near the famous Butchart Gardens. The friends devoured several power bars and guzzled water all the while tuning in to the drone that surrounded them. Jesse signalled to go back. Off they went. The wind pushed at them so they had to paddle with more resolution. By the time the landing at Brentwood Bay was in sight, they were exhausted. It was a superb day undisturbed by the cell phone Gibson had deliberately left behind on the dresser. The grin on his face as he dragged his kayak onto the wharf was proof of his 'Don't Care' attitude. He was overwhelmed with the week's events. Something about being outside vaporized the disquiet. They walked up the incline together, promising another day of kayaking tomorrow.

Katherine's SUV wasn't in the driveway, so the doubt that had sprung up was spurious. When his wife returned home, he took the phone off the hook and shut down his cell. It was a rebellious move that he seldom did, but he needed an entire carefree night with his wife.

* * *

Sunday was an echo of Saturday. Gibson met Jesse at the café. After a shot of caffeine, they strolled lazily to their boats confident of the day. They headed north this time, zigzagging in and out of the coastline. Both men were chattier today, babbling about new gear and equipment. Gibson let the last of his apprehension melt away as the hours passed by, pleasantly paddling his trusted kayak. The sun was intense in the sky and beating down on them as they veered toward home at the halfway mark. Jesse picked up the pace, propelling himself to the limit. Gibson followed. His muscles weakened and his lungs burned. All he wanted to do was stop and catch his breath. Gibson hit the dreaded wall and pressed on, letting the throbbing wash over him. They lay on the dock, tension from their exertion melting into the hard surface—slow, smooth breathing restored. They bumped fists.

Gibson headed home. His mouth watered the moment he swung open the door. The rich aroma of roast beef wafted down the hallway and beckoned him to the kitchen. The music was low. Katherine sat at the table, tapping a foot to the easy beat. A random birdsong floated through the crack of the open window.

"Ten minutes." Her smile was sweet with a faint curve of the lips.

Later they relaxed on the couch, fire throwing warmth into the room. Katherine discussed her disintegration in the hallway, happy to expel her demons. Just as Gibson had driven through a physical barrier that afternoon, Katherine had pushed through a mental block the other day. Youthful self-assurance put rosy dots of colour on her cheeks and a sparkle in her eyes. Hope whispered in her ear. Would she pass the exam and secure the coveted diploma? Gibson braced himself against any other conclusion.

Chapter 26

How was it that Mondays always rolled around so fast? Still, Gibson considered himself fortunate. Not every case came with weekends off. Katherine had been more relaxed than normal, although she was prickly. She had completed her final exam, but now the wait for the results gnawed on her nerves—and his. He stood at the front window sipping his first coffee of the day and gazed at the bay shimmering in the sunlight. It was another glorious fall morning with a cloudless sky. He walked back to the kitchen and watched Katherine pottering around in her greenhouse. It was time to regroup. He headed out, glancing once more at the ocean and all its potentials. He drove through his little village and hit the freeway, joining the long lines of vehicles going into the city.

Gibson had a tough job finding a parking space on the street so he headed to the underground garage. He slogged up the steps, gave a wave to the receptionist behind the security counter and trudged on to the next floor. Scottie was in her office bent over a pile of folders scattered across her desk.

"Hey."

Scottie looked up and fell back in her chair, tossing a pen on top of the papers. She stretched her legs out and stifled a yawn with her hand.

"I hate paperwork."

Gibson hung onto the doorframe as he leaned into the room and nodded. He knew Scottie had spent countless hours on Friday writing the reports, perusing each page to ensure the details were correct. The chief was a stickler for accuracy. The Crown Attorney had hammered that home after a ruined trial last year. An indiscretion in a detective's statement had blown the case into smithereens.

"Did you find out anything about either the homeless guy or the dog walker?"

"No. I got hung up on this," Scottie said and picked up a document. She was ruffled.

"The chief. You know."

"Yeah," Gibson quirked an eyebrow and smiled. "Thanks for covering for me." Scottie understood his situation at home with Katherine. Gibson never had to solicit help.

She shrugged it off.

"The bully factor is out. Right?"

"Yes. I suppose." He grudgingly conceded on that point. Tim was in the clear. Doesn't mean he's not a bully, he thought to himself, not daring to voice that to Scottie. He didn't need a 'told you so'.

"What an ass. That's for sure." Scottie laughed. She watched him teeter on dark emotions and changed the subject. "So, money?"

"Gunner and Na are still checking the cash trail," Gibson said. "Too bad we can't bring Tony down for sexual improprieties." He studied the ceiling, his jaw thrust forward.

"We know Jeff gains financially from Robbie's death." She motioned her partner into her office.

Gibson sat in the solitary chair in front of her desk. He crossed his legs. His right hand drummed a song he had heard on the drive in.

"The chief feels strongly about the money motive. Could we put some pressure on Jeff? He seems to be the most promising person at this point. What have we got?"

Scottie pulled a journal out of her pocket and flipped through several pages. She tapped the book and put it away.

"He doesn't have an alibi."

Gibson's thought as well—alibis. He had pursued the investigation in a linear motion, bent on pursuing the bully. Now each person's whereabouts had to be made clear. It was obvious they had overlooked a detail. Not having an alibi didn't make a person guilty, but it did eliminate the individual as a suspect.

"Ellen's is solid." Gibson pushed back in the chair, extending his legs out.

"Who else?"

"Nick." Scottie closed her eyes momentarily. "And Tony. We have to recheck everybody."

Gibson blew out a loud sigh, making that rude noise with his lips again.

Scottie looked up, shocked at her boss's lack of finesse, not in character.

"It's getting to me," was his only comeback.

"I hear you."

"The guys at the safety seminar," he continued.

"That's another big black hole," Scottie agreed.

They sat quietly, each in their deliberations. Gibson thought they had let their guard down. Apparently so did Scottie because she spoke up, mirroring his sentiments.

"Okay, we really didn't pin that meeting down. Did we? And I'd like to scout out that homeless guy." Scottie stopped to think it over. "Give me one day to find him. Somehow he must be connected to this."

"Sure," Gibson agreed. "The jacket won't help us."

"Nope."

"Let's get a coffee."

They walked down to the employee restaurant on the first floor. The place was full of the chatter of detectives, deafening in the low-ceilinged room. Gibson felt restless and sat quietly. He had been unfocused all week by Katherine, the exam and the panic attack. Was he so preoccupied he had stopped doing his job well? He breathed in. Then let out another moan. Scottie left him to his musings and enjoyed an egg salad sandwich with her drink. The prattle at a table diagonal to them distracted him. He tilted his head at a sharp angle and twitched his lips upward. What had he overheard? Old man and a dog. Run over. His ears pricked up when he heard it happened at the university. Was it their dog walker? That would be a coincidence. He glanced over at Scottie and noticed the chatter had caught her interest too. She raised her eyebrows, motioned her chin in question to the group of officers.

"Check it out."

"Yes, sounds like our guy."

After their break, they moved out in opposite ways. Gibson drove over to the maintenance shed to see about the trucks. He had left in a rush on Friday and neglected to find out about the fleet protocol. He parked along the curb and headed for the workshop. AJ was busy at his work bench. He saw Gibson enter, so he put down his hammer and removed his gloves.

"What's up?"

"Who gets a vehicle? Not for work but for personal use."

"Both the supervisor and foremen take a truck home." AJ paused, running his hand across the still tender gash. "Whoever's on call takes one as well."

"Who was it that weekend?" Gibson's eyebrows arched.

"David."

Gibson's posture stiffened. He had let David's alibi slide. A visit to Jackie was in order. He leaned his hip against the workbench trying to think this through.

"What about the keys? Especially to the back." He pointed to the rear.

"Everybody in the yard has a full set for all the doors. We rotate the on-call work. It's easier that way."

Dead end. Access for all. Damn. There was a big whoosh of cool air. A tall, gangly fellow stepped into the room letting the door slam behind him. He looked at both men and smiled. AJ introduced.

"Meet Keith."

The illusive assistant supervisor darted his eyes around the shop. Perfect. Gibson needed to pin down the movements of everyone at the meeting. This man would know. Keith had the best view that morning standing at the front. Gibson wanted everything. Who got up? Who left? How long were they gone?

"I don't know." Keith pursed his lips together, shaking his head back and forth in a constant motion at the questions Gibson fired at him.

It was hopeless. The man was no help at all. It had been his first time running a meeting, and he was nervous. He didn't notice anyone come or go. Gibson continued to be disappointed. No confirmation of anybody's movement. What was wrong with the people here? But still, it was a long shot. Not sufficient time to run across the courtyard, kill someone and make it back—no blood, not breathing hard. But certainly time enough to see something. Gibson was frustrated. He would arrange for Na to set up a fresh round of interviews. It would get sorted or…? Or what?

He left the building and sat in the F150, his eyes fixed inwards. He lowered the window and filled his lungs with the freshness before firing up the engine. It roared to life with one turn of the key. He headed out of the university grounds and took a right to Foul Bay Road. When he got to the house, he saw a white pickup truck parked in the driveway with some advertising on the side panels. He rapped on the door loudly. Jeff answered after a few minutes, opening the door only a crack. Gibson could see his dirty T-shirt and baggy jogging pants. As if Jeff ever jogged. What was wrong with him? Where was this cynicism coming from? He needed a holiday—at the least a scoot around the bay. Was it only Monday?

"Is that your vehicle?"

"Yeah."

"What do you do for a living?" Gibson asked, although he had read the sign on the side panel.

"A painting contractor," Jeff said. "Not much work in the winter."

"I haven't seen your truck before. Where is it usually parked?"

"My friend borrowed it last week. To get firewood."

"Person's name?"

Jeff gave him a name. Gibson jotted it down in his notebook with a big question mark. He would definitely follow up.

"Is that it?" Jeff held onto the door tightly. There would be no invite into the house today. Gibson leaned in and caught a whiff of something pungent—weed.

"You don't have an alibi."

All he got in reply was a twisted grin.

"Did anyone see you that morning?"

"What?"

"You heard me." Gibson tapped the pad with his pen. "It's going to be a problem for you."

Jeff gave him a last defiant glare and slammed the door shut.

Chapter 27

Gibson walked through the empty detective agency and opened the door to his office. He sat at his desk, shuffling through some papers. It may have been another sun-drenched day but his disposition was anything but sunny. The previous day hadn't brought any clarity to the investigation. Everything had bogged down since Tim had been cleared of suspicion. He began reworking the evidence painstakingly, taking great care over each minor factor. He flipped through his notebook, page by page. Something would show up, some trivial detail that would clinch the case. He had honed in on one individual and sought to make the facts fit because of his own biases. When would he quit beating himself up over that?

Reading all morning in the quiet room had caused his muscles to cramp. Gibson stood up to stretch, stepping over to the window. The sun was at its zenith. Rays glittered on the ocean below, some light reaching the bottomless depths, some reflecting off the crystal water. Golden energy filled the sky with an intrinsic luminosity. Blue skies prevailed. He glanced down to the pavement and watched a group of bikers cycling to the park. He issued a short, mirthless laugh and turned from the view.

With a strategy for the afternoon, Gibson stopped at the Ottiva for lunch first. He enjoyed a latte and a chicken salad. The sandwich was prepared with bread baked that morning. He had smelled the comforting aroma upon entering the café, making his mouth water in anticipation. The nose had not failed him. The meal was exceptional. He finished up and left the restaurant. He was in a better mood. Gibson got back into his truck and made his way to Cordova Bay. The street followed the shoreline for a few kilometres so he lowered his window to the salty air—wonderfully refreshing.

At the maintenance shed he found out that Nick had called in sick. Gibson needed Kim's last name. He parked beside the massive hedge that fronted the house and strolled along the curved sidewalk to the entrance. It was a tidy yard with all the leaves raked, grass cut low for the winter and the evergreen trimmed. He paused on the porch and listened for sounds inside before he knocked. It was several minutes before he detected footsteps coming, and the door lurched wide.

"Hi. Not feeling well."

Nick glared at him and swung away. He gestured with a backward wave of his hand for Gibson to follow. The living room wasn't as spruce as it had been at his initial visit. It seemed bleak and dismal. Several dirty mugs and plates were littering the side tables. Newspapers were strewn on the floor. Nick plunked himself into a recliner.

"Where's Susan?" Gibson asked.

"She left to visit her mom," he said. His shoulders slumped and his eyes constricted with a mournful gaze. "And the kids."

"What's going on?"

"She suspects something."

"That you killed Robbie?"

"No!" Nick yelled as he bolted out of his chair. He paced up and down at the bay window, fists clenched by his side. His cheeks flushed scarlet and roasted hot. He peered sideways at Gibson and sat down, eyes cast to the ground.

Gibson picked an armchair opposite him, leaned forward and completed the thought for him. "Your cheating."

"Maybe. What's it to you?"

Gibson reached into his upper pocket, plucked out the Facebook photo and extended it to him.

"Is that you?"

"No." Nick thrust the image away.

"You and Robbie argued."

"No!"

Gibson pressed on.

"A lover's quarrel?" If that had led to murder was what he was pondering—maybe even a lover's triangle somewhere in there.

"Are you insane?" Nick shrieked, vaulting out of his chair again. "Nothing is going on."

"Something's going on." He watched Nick's pale skin turn from a ghastly white to a shade of ghost.

Gibson knew he wasn't getting any more out of him today so he left the man to brood and slipped out. He hopped into his truck and decided to drive the back route to Brentwood Bay. It was a quick route that only the locals knew. He crossed the highway and took Keating over to Clarke. The blacktop road dropped to the harbour where a small ferry carried passengers and vehicles across the inlet to Mills Bay. David lived about halfway down the slope. He parked on the boulevard opposite the two-storey dwelling. It had brick cladding on the front with white siding and louvered shutters by the small windows. The brown asphalt roof had several angles with a dormer facing south. Five deciduous saplings planted on the lawn would grow into large trees one day and conceal the house from the street and the sun in the summer.

He glanced down the side of the house. There weren't any vehicles visible, but there might be one in the garage at the bottom of the drive. He couldn't tell because the walls there had no windows. It was doubtful that Jackie was home. Maybe he should have phoned first. He walked along the sidewalk to a porch. The lady, bundled in several layers of clothing, was raking up the last of the pin oak leaves next door. She flipped her palm up in a cordial wave. Gibson gestured back. An ornamental knocker on the frame looked unused so he buzzed the bell and waited. The door was painted the charcoal of a winter's sky, same as the shutters. It swung open with a rustle of air. An olive-skinned lady peered at him. She looked casual in a yellow and blue Fair Isle sweater with tight jeans and multi-coloured woollen socks on her petite feet.

"Hi. Inspector Gibson." He flashed his badge.

"Yes. How can I help you?"

"When we spoke on the phone the other day, you told me David left for work at six-thirty. I just want to confirm that time."

"I don't know what else to say," Jackie said. "Like I told you, it's always the same time."

"Did you actually see him leave that morning?"

"I slept in. So no, but our neighbour notices when he leaves."

"What do you mean?"

"David's jeep is noisy. I'm positive he wakes up most of the district at dawn."

"The lady raking next door?"

"Yes."

Gibson thanked her and stepped outside. He walked over to the fence and watched the lady pile leaves into gigantic heaps. She grabbed a load and wrestled it into a plastic bag. When she spun around, she noticed him standing there.

"Hi. May I ask you a few things?" He showed his badge.

"How can I help?" Her skin was blotchy from the cold damp air.

"Tell me about the Jeep."

"Why? Are you going to arrest David for not having a muffler?" Small dimples formed on her cheeks when she smiled.

"Last Monday, did you see him leave for work?" He wasn't sure what she meant.

"Like clockwork. He's my alarm clock. First the jeep shutters and rattles because it doesn't start right away. Then it fires up with a roar. David pumps the gas a few times and off he goes. Under my bedroom window." She paused and pointed behind her. "Six-thirty on the dot, for six years."

"No doubt about last Monday."

"Not at all. He left at six-thirty."

Gibson returned to his truck to consider his next move. He was writing this information in his journal when his cell buzzed. It was Katherine.

"I passed with honours."

He could sense her breathlessness as she talked. He had a desire to see her. He could feel joy pass through him like an ocean wave washing on the shore.

"I'll be home in a minute."

There was a hiss down the line. Katherine was gone. He fired up the engine and was about to pull from the curb when his phone sounded.

"Gibson."

It was Scottie. He turned off the ignition.

"I've been with Liam," she said. "The dog walker."

Gibson grunted.

"He stepped off the sidewalk at a crosswalk and a truck almost ran him over."

"Lucky he wasn't hit."

"No kidding. But he stumbled on the pavement and broke his arm. The driver took off. But he figured the guy hadn't seen him because there aren't many street lights. He usually wore reflective clothing and a flasher on his dog's collar but he was in a hurry that morning. It happened so fast that he didn't get a good look at the truck."

"That's too bad."

"I took him to the maintenance yard. He didn't recognize the truck as one of them. You know the truck he saw Monday morning."

"Not surprised."

Scottie gave a gruff laugh. Gibson perceived there was further news.

"We went to Jeff's house. Liam thought it could be the truck he had seen."

"How confident was he?" Gibson asked.

"Pretty sure." She blew out a sigh.

"Not good enough. The Crown Attorney would howl at us."

"Yeah, it's lame. But maybe it all adds up. With the bat. The money…" She hesitated.

"Same with Nick. Something there but not. Probably nothing to do with us," Gibson said.

There was no feedback from Scottie.

"Ah, shit. I forgot to ask him about Kim. Where's my head these days?" Gibson said.

Scottie grunted. Was she morphing into her boss with all the body noises?

"I'm calling it a day. See you tomorrow." All at once he felt exhausted.

Chapter 28

The sky was an unbroken sea of faded blue. Muted pinks and oranges piled on top of each other as the sun hit the horizon. Gibson was halfway up the island to Duncan. He had received an unexpected call about a missing girl. The Vancouver Island Integrated Major Crimes Unit's jurisdiction extended as far north as Nanaimo. Any incident of kidnapping, lost children or other serious crime within these boundaries would reach down to Gibson and his squad for cooperation. They needed it now. He listened to the radio as he drove, strumming his fingers on the steering wheel. He shouldn't be happy, but it was nice to leave his own case behind for a while. Scottie had several details to attend to so he took it upon himself to go. Well, the boss had suggested it. Traffic was substantial in the opposite direction with commuters heading into Victoria. His side of the highway was clear sailing. He hit two traffic lights on the way up. He pulled into the Royal Canadian Mounted Police (RCMP) Department on Sheldon Avenue by eight o'clock. The ever-changing sky had darkened to a robin's egg blue.

The station was a modern low-slung building built of concrete with long, narrow windows every three metres inset deeply into the thick walls. The desk sergeant was missing from behind the reception counter. Just a couple of flags and a portrait stood guard. The sound of braying phones could be heard from somewhere within the building. Gibson followed the deafening chatter down a wide flight of stairs to a tight corridor, made even more constricted by the number of people milling around. The loudest noise was coming from a set of open double doors near the end. He made his way through the commotion and stood at the entrance of a large conference room. Inside, there was a flurry of activity.

A huge map pinned to a wall was pierced with different coloured tacks. A sharpie divided the map into sections with notations beside each area. There were fewer crossed out spaces than checked marked ones. Makeshift tables and old school-like desks were shoved into the centre with people sitting at most of the spots. Their faces were stern and their heads pressed into phones, trying to hear over the din. The voices were flat and subdued, barely perceptible. Everything echoed against the walls. Each call answered was a chance—a possible crack in the case.

At the centre of activity soaring above the assembly was Chief Superintendent Stu Kelly, authoritative and self-confident. He noticed Gibson's arrival as soon as he stepped foot in the room. That awareness to detail had made scaling the corporate ladder a sure bet for Kelly. They were friends and had worked on several situations together, always amid a tragedy. The chief gave him a hearty handshake but lips compressed white told the truth of the situation. Without fuss Kelly provided him the grim details, and then pointed to one of the rickety desks for him to set up shop.

The desk was too small for Gibson so he squeezed in as far as he could and let his legs stretch out. The little girl missing would be way more uncomfortable than him. He spent most of the day on the phone taking tips from the public. He consulted with the men who scoured the woodlands, the meadows and the abandoned buildings. When the phones stopped ringing so insistently, he joined the search outside. He became one of the guys rushing in and out of the building, marking where he had been and where he needed to go next. The circle on the map grew wider as the day grew longer. Back at his appointed desk inbetween the hunt, he guzzled copious amounts of coffee to sustain his energy level. But as time crawled on for the lost minor and flew by for the rescuers, Gibson—exhausted, depleted—felt bogged down in the quagmire. He glanced around at the haggard expressions, the distressed eyes and the slumped bodies. But it was the continual nervous tapping of fingers and pencils resonating through the room that conveyed despair the most. Time—it was all about time. He knew it and the faces surrounding him proved they perceived it too. The initial period was crucial if they were to locate the child. He plowed on.

Finally someone brought in sandwiches causing a traffic jam at a table in the corridor. Hunger was rampant and they consumed trays of food within minutes—fear and anxiety creating a desire to replenish.

Ten hours passed by, then twelve. The sun had left an hour ago, the black desolation of night closing in. As the sky deepened, the harvest moon cast luminous rays of silver onto the dark grounds. Nobody wanted to give up.

Chief Kelly rubbed his forehead and sucked in some air. He stood up and called for everyone's attention. Bleary eyes stared up at him.

"Okay, everyone. It's late. We're all tired."

There was an audible sigh, but no one objected.

"We'll leave a skeleton crew for the phones." Kelly pointed to a few men who had joined the rescue party later in the day. "The rest of you, go. Get some sleep."

Gibson followed the crowd out the door and headed to a motel. He didn't want to talk to anybody—just

Katherine. He kept it simple. He kept most of it to himself. But hearing her voice was enough.

* * *

Gibson was up early. The sun was just peeking over the hilltop. He squared his shoulders and put on a brave face. These cases were worse than murders. He wondered if Scottie was making any progress. She would only call if she actually had a killer in handcuffs. A child's life was at stake here. He entered the hall and took his seat. The faces around him were grim—hope almost lost. He stayed at his station answering phones for hours—six, eight. All at once someone yelled and leaped upon a wooden bench. The man held up his fist for stillness. The throng paused what they were working on and turned toward the shout. Palms covered the mouthpieces of phones, pens stopped scribbling on notepads and chalk on blackboards froze mid-sentence. There was a collective intake of breath. Everyone stared at the individual who had barked out for attention. A phone was pressed to his ear. His hand remained paralyzed over his shoulder as he listened. A smile broke his sullen face. His lips curved up into a broad ear-to-ear grin. It was funny to see a grown man giggle. Slow drops of pent up moisture ran from his emotional and unblinking eyes. He hung up. A lungful of air rushed out his mouth in a whoosh.

"We found Gracie!" he roared, then collapsed in his chair.

It took a minute for the announcement to register.

"Hurrah!" A harmony of voices bellowed out from the enthusiastic gathering. Bountiful tears spilled down cheeks. People gripped their neighbour in strong hugs with soundless sobs. Thin laughter and silent prayers spread across the town. Frequently the outcome was unsuccessful. Today the sun had shone on their efforts. How the child had survived the cold night alone Gibson didn't know.

Wasn't sure he wanted to know. It only mattered that she had.

He joined in the celebration, drained and emotional. All the members of the force and volunteers were equally diminished. Chief Kelly patted him on the back as the men and women crowded close. Someone cracked open the whiskey. He slipped out and made the long drive home.

* * *

Scottie had spent an arduous time at the maintenance shed, chatting, interviewing and working over particulars. Na ran second shotgun—zilch. There was no agreement on anybody leaving the meeting. No one saw AJ's attacker. What homeless man? Didn't see a thing? Round and round they spun seeking the weak link, but something sealed the men's lips. There was nothing to be discovered. Who were they protecting? Or were they all innocent?

After two days, Na was left exhausted by the experience. Scottie would never give up.

Chapter 29

It was a sunny day, cooler with a slight breeze from the Northeast. Gibson stood at the window when Scottie placed her grip on the door frame and snooped around the corner.

"Wasn't sure you'd be here," she said in response to her partner's quizzical expression.

"It was dreadful. But they found the girl." He ambled across the office and perched in his chair. He pulled out a lower drawer, planted his feet on top and leaned back into his seat. She gave him a progress report. His cell buzzed. He plucked up the receiver.

"Gibson."

The chief was on the other end so he punched another button.

"Give me an update," he bellowed.

"Scottie's here too." Letting the chief know he was on speaker phone. They gave him the latest.

"Keep at it." Rex muttered. "They need you in Duncan again."

Gibson frowned. How would they ever get their case solved? As soon as he put the phone in its cradle, a second call came in.

"Got something I think would interest you," Gunner said. "The dealership is repossessing Jeff's new work vehicle."

Gunner had been diligent in his efforts to scout out more reasons to consider Jeff. They thanked him for his painstaking digging into the finances. The two detectives looked at each other. Scottie slapped the desk and crinkled her eyes. Finally something they could touch.

"Let's get our reports caught up today before I leave." He checked his watch. "Two hours and I'll head out."

"Sure. But I still haven't caught up with the camp guys."

"Why don't you go later this afternoon?" Gibson said.

"You're right. The men split before I get there in the morning."

"Put together all you can on Jeff. Go over everything Gunner has found out so far."

"Okay. He definitely seems suspicious," Scottie replied.

"We don't have enough to do anything about it yet."

"I know."

Gibson was so exhausted from the missing child case that he almost fell asleep at his desk. He put down his paperwork and stretched out on the couch for a little nap.

* * *

Scottie slipped out late in the afternoon to scout out the camp. As she strolled over the soggy lawn, she could feel water seeping through her shoes. Damn. But that was okay because this time she got lucky. There was a ring of guys squatted on discarded crates and decayed logs. No one moved when she came into the clearing. An individual with black and yellow marks on his cheeks glared as she approached. The man remained still, a glower on his face and fury in his empty stare.

"I've been looking for you," she said. "What happened?"

He rolled his swollen eyes in resentment, as reluctant to talk as his fellow campers were. His trembling chin and slouched shoulders relayed the hurt he had endured from the thumping.

"I got beat up. What do you think?"

Scottie halted, surprised that he had answered her at all. She waited to hear more.

"Why do you care?" he asked angrily. Mumbles of discontent floated through the men.

"Were you involved with the murder?" She was ready to snatch the guy if he attempted to do a runner, although he didn't look like he could even walk that well. She relaxed.

"He got beat up for carrying too much cash," a man said and laughed gruffly.

"He was with us when that person was murdered," echoed another.

They hollered in unison. Scottie escaped the circle and trotted back across the grass to her vehicle. Scratch out that one, she thought as she drove home.

* * *

Gibson got up and felt a little better. He looked into Scottie's office, but she was gone. After a glance at his watch, he realized he should be on his way. He had slept longer than he had wanted to, and he had to head home first. Katherine was busy in the kitchen making him a snack to take on the road. He packed the few things he needed into a small black duffle bag. At the last moment, he tossed in the book he had left on the night stand—its page marked in the same spot for two days. Maybe he would get a chance to read a bit more. He heard the finches chirping so he headed to the dining room. His wife sat at the table with his snack in a paper bag on the table. Beside it rested an empty picture frame all shiny and new. The diploma that Katherine had earned and would receive in a pompous ceremony the following week, would find its place within the frame and be hung on the wall in the den. She smiled warmly and fingered the cool metal, happy in her own fashion. Her usual abandonment issues were tucked away in a closet somewhere for now.

Gibson glanced at his watch for the hundredth time today.

"Gotta go." He grabbed the bag and hurried down the hallway, realizing the next ferry would be docking soon. That meant the highways would be crowded and the going slow. Every hour on the hour. It was always a matter of timing not to get stuck in the lines.

"Ferry traffic."

"Okay. See you in two days."

Gibson watched as she blew a kiss through the window. He whipped out of the sleepy village to the busy highway. The trip to Duncan was boring, but he made it in pretty good time. He headed to the same RCMP station that he had been to not that many days ago.

Everything seemed quieter when he entered the building. Chief Kelly sat at a computer at someone else's desk. The printer behind him was churning out page after page. They made a crackling sound as they fell to the floor. The chief got up and gathered them into a nice neat pile.

"Hey. Take a seat. Sorry we had to call for help so soon."

"That's okay." Gibson said it, but he wasn't sure he meant it. He had so much on his plate at home.

Kelly gave him the gist of the problem he was up against. This time it was an attempted murder case. Thank god it wasn't another child. He didn't think he could handle another case like that so soon. This new case was anything but a slam dunk. The police knew who the perpetrator was, but they needed help with collecting evidence. And Gibson was good at that.

"Could you give me two days?" Kelly handed him the neat pile of paper.

"Okay." The stack was three inches thick.

"Pick any desk you want. At least the desks in here are adult size." Kelly laughed.

Gibson had a lot of reading to do before he could even think about what direction to take. He plugged away until his eyes were sore. An owl hooted somewhere in the distance. He looked out the window to a yellowish light from the sodium lamps in the parking lot. Darkness had crept in quietly while he was immersed in the pages. He left the material with the desk sergeant and went to the same motel. It was midnight by the time he lay on the bed. His eyelids fluttered. He was buried in sleep with the book open on his lap at the same page.

* * *

The next morning Gibson went to the closest café for breakfast. He drank coffee until he felt the kick of the caffeine. He left the restaurant with an extra large to go. The sky was a clear blue with white and fluffy clouds making an escape to the east on a persistent breeze. That meant sunny weather coming soon. He walked over to the station, but Kelly wasn't there. He slogged away at the files, making notations on a separate pad. Lunch time rolled around and the chief hadn't made an appearance yet. He toiled on some more. His cell chirped several times during the day, but he ignored most of the calls. After the fourth buzz, he turned off his phone. It was hard enough to get through this stuff without all the interruptions. Scottie knew better than to harass him, but she had called him twice already. She would have to figure out whatever was bugging her on her own.

He was getting a headache from squinting at the bright sheets of paper. He packed it in for the day without seeing anybody except for the sergeant. Most of the officers were on surveillance, hanging out from doorways and parked vehicles, waiting for their guy to make his first mistake. The setting sun exploded into a tangerine hue before the inky skies overtook it. The night air was chilly and the sky a million glimmers of light. At the motel, he didn't bother to pick up his book, but stared at his phone. He fell asleep before calling his wife.

The next morning Gibson walked down the street with a sun that warmed his body, but not his mood. White birds high in the sky glided on the thermals in long arcs. His cell vibrated in his pocket.

"Gibson."

"Hello, it's me. Have you forgotten?" Katherine asked.

"I have not forgotten. I will be home tonight no matter what."

They chatted for a few minutes while he walked down the pavement. The contralto of her voice lifted his gloom. She sang as sweetly as her beloved finches. The last of the grey baleful clouds got chased away. Kelly was at the reception counter when he arrived at the station.

"I have a few more things for you here." He handed over a small folder. "I think something in here will click with something in the papers I gave you the other day."

"Okay."

"Has anything twigged at all?" Kelly grimaced. He didn't want to push.

"Yes, as a matter of fact. There was something I want to look at again." Gibson had that niggle in the back of his thoughts that often turned a blurry black and white picture into a high definition movie. "Give me a few hours."

He sat back down at the desk and decided to look in the binder first. Something caught his eye. Something that scratched that niggle. He worked at his desk for most of the morning, checking and double-checking his facts. He thought he was close. And then it came to him. He got the desk sergeant to call up Kelly. The chief arrived just after lunch. They went over everything and agreed that the thing he found would do it. It was so simple in the end. They found the incriminating evidence on the guy's Facebook. What a laugh.

Sunday rolled around to a happy ending—for Gibson. He got to go home. Not so much for the suspect. He got to go to jail.

Gibson phoned Scottie on his way down the highway.

"I'm done here. Meet up with you tomorrow. We have to get on with it before all is lost."

"You bet. Nothing happened here." A faint tone of disappointment crept into her voice.

* * *

Monday morning the darkened clouds fought with the sky for priority. They skittered across the blue and blocked out the sun. Where the hell did they come from? It was a typical autumn morning—more white than blue.

"Hey." Scottie slumped into a chair at Gibson's desk. "I'm ready for the next round."

"Me too."

"Get Gunner in here. Let's see what we have."

Scottie took off across the hallway and nabbed the constable.

"Jeff owes money. Lots of it. His business is failing too." Gunner placed a folder on the desk. "It's all in here."

"Okay. That gives us something."

After the constable headed back to his office, the two detectives knew they had better find a money trail to somebody before the chief called again. So they buried their heads into more paperwork, trying to snuff out what they could without warrants. That would come later when they had probable cause. It was a balancing act with the judges and the Crown Attorney.

"I give up. Let's kick some ass instead." Gibson threw back his head in a fit of laugher, tears running down his cheeks.

"Are you losing it?" Scottie stared at him.

"No. I'm just in a good mood. Tomorrow is Katherine's graduation." Gibson beamed. "That's where I'll be."

"Oh, so you want me to kick ass."

"Right."

"Want me to haul Jeff into the station tomorrow?" she asked. "He'll be more cooperative in an interview room."

"The small, stuffy one." Gibson chuckled.

Scottie didn't comment, but she put on her Cheshire smile.

"Depending on how that goes, bring Nick in after that," Gibson paused. "Even Jason. None of these guys has a credible alibi. Let's squeeze them. We're running out of time."

"Let's get tough."

They bumped fists.

Chapter 30

Katherine's smooth, clear notes rose above the rich vibrato of the violin, its raw and harrowing undertones in contrast to her sweet and pure voice. Birdsong flowed freely through the open window. The aria beckoned Gibson. Its gradual crescendo was almost a summons. He glided down the hallway in stocking feet, his footfalls making no sound at all. He watched her dance with liquid grace across the tile floor. Her hair was lazily ruffled. The warm chestnut hues had a hint of red when the sunlight came in at just the right angle. Today was her moment. After so many years and considerable anguish, she had reached the pinnacle of her dreams. She whirled around and saw him leaning against the door frame. She let her smile widen into a brilliant grin. A sparkle that had started at the corner of her mouth advanced upwards to her brown eyes. He shifted toward her and pressed his torso into hers. Her body was supple. She yielded to his touch. He skimmed his lips against her willing mouth. He could feel her aura of tranquillity like a thin veil of translucent colour.

In their surreal sway, only a sharp knock on the door could have brought them back. Gibson lingered for barely a moment before he released his hold. He pulled the door open to a grinning Andrew who stood on the porch with his hands behind his back.

"We just made a pot of coffee." A blush hid behind Gibson's fading tan.

"We should go to the café," Andrew said. "My sister needs to do something with her hair."

"Bum." Katherine poked his shoulder. She closed the door softly behind them.

The sun shone with an autumn dullness that warned of winter coming. The air was crisp with a bite of cool from the ocean and a faint woody fragrance of fireplace smoke. They drifted down the ramp to the Seaside Café. Gibson was surprised his buddy wasn't in the usual spot by the window. The waitress brought over two coffees before she was asked.

"Jesse left in his kayak early."

"Lucky guy."

She laughed and spun away at the tone of a bell chiming.

Gibson fingered his mug absent-mindedly, peering into the depth of the liquid.

"May I finish my story from the other day?"

Andrew nodded.

"My brother died when we were teenagers." He stared into the past. Trees, tire swings and swimming pools. "I was a teenager. Richard was twelve."

Andrew sat still.

"While he was being bullied, I was trying to pick up girls. He was my little brother so I ignored him. Stupid me." Gibson shrugged.

Andrew wanted to reach out and bring light where there was darkness.

"Richard committed suicide."

A small squeal escaped from Andrew. He sucked in his breath and splayed his fingers out in a fan against his chest, feeling the strong beat of his existence drumming rapidly.

"I wish I had listened. I should have believed him." Gibson felt the pain. "My mother…she wasn't there anymore, not in spirit. Just a meaningless passing of time." The thoughts that followed he kept to himself because it was too much to share. Not even now, not ever. The grief had changed his dad too. His eyes had sunk into his face, had lost their spark. Did his dad drink more? He hid it well. Gibson dropped his head into his palms and squeezed back the tears that took cover behind his smiling eyes. The longing for what could have been never leaving his heart.

Andrew remained silent.

"I've never revealed my secret," he said.

Andrew waited.

"Not even to Katherine." Gibson's shaky chuckle broke the uneasiness. "Don't tell her."

"I won't. I promise."

"Hopefully one day we'll be old men sharing a bench and a coffee." Gibson shoved the sorrow back in its place. The steam that had arisen from his coffee had disappeared long ago, when he had drifted to another time and place. Through the window, he saw the sun was at its zenith, tracking lower in the sky than in the summer. What warmth it shed had radiated outwards and touched him. But the hot sun was powerless to eclipse the compassion he felt toward Andrew. And Andrew to him.

They walked back to the house different men.

Katherine bounced to the front when she heard the door slam. She blushed, enhancing the bloom on her cheeks. Usually she hid from the limelight, but today she bathed in its luminescence.

Gibson dressed quickly and rejoined his companions.

"Ready?"

They piled into the truck and headed for the university. Gibson hit the freeway and then took the off-ramp at McKenzie. The traffic was light, and shortly they arrived. He dropped them at the main entrance so he could hunt for a parking spot. It was a big day for many graduating students and their families. He circled farther and farther from the building in search of a vacant space. He got lucky. He tapped his upper pocket to make sure the gift for Katherine was secure. He jumped out and trekked it back to the auditorium. The high-ceilinged room was abuzz with gaiety intermingled with elation. The front ten rows were reserved for the graduates. He spotted his wife sitting in the third row with her chin held high and her hands poised on her lap. Relaxed. Andrew was on the left side of the room and waved him over. Gibson made his way through the slow-moving crowd and plunked down on a folded chair. Heather had beat him there and was already seated. She had her legs crossed with fingers intertwined over one knee.

Faculty clad in academic regalia were settled in their assigned chairs on stage. The president climbed up the low steps and strode over to the podium. She adjusted the medallion on her blazer and stepped up to the microphone.

"Could everybody quiet down, and we'll begin the ceremony?"

The buzz in the air fell as all attention shifted to the dais. In reverence of the ritual observances, they quieted to coughing or clearing of the throat. The president's speech filled with words of wisdom and intermingled with humour ended with a thunderous clapping. The robed graduates walked in procession up the steps and across the lengthy platform to be awarded their papers and congratulations. Gibson anticipated Katherine's turn with euphoria. He held onto Heather's hand, his own palms damp. As the Dean of Business placed the diploma in Katherine's outstretched palm, some erroneous element swirled into his mind like ripples on the water that show where the danger lies. It wasn't about Katherine this time but everything to do with murder.

Gibson released his hold on Heather and perched on the edge of his seat, impatient to rush out. Katherine turned. Her lit face was staggering. It pushed him back into his chair. He pulled out his cell and texted Scottie with brief directions. He crossed and uncrossed his legs nervously, looking at his phone too many times. He tried to focus his attention back to Katherine. She cranked her neck and peered over the crowd to find her man. Gibson did not let her down. He waved energetically to draw her in his direction. They locked eyes. Hers were twinkling. He struggled to suppress the anxiety in his. Another hour passed before hats flew in the air, some reaching the ceiling. Katherine approached them, her body quivering with pride. Even the news that he would have to leave didn't hinder her delight. He left Andrew to accompany the ladies to the luncheon and dashed out to his truck. As he was jogging through the parking lot, his cell rang.

"Gibson."

"You're right," Scottie said.

"Okay. I'll go over to the college." He bulldozed his way across town through heavy gridlock and congestion at every crossroad and traffic light. At the administrative office, he found a knowledgeable person amenable to searching through years of files. Among the vast data banks, Gibson found the verification that he had expected.

Meanwhile Scottie headed to Ottiva to sort through the files that she had been assigned. She hunched over her plate, biting into the sandwich absent-mindedly and taking sips of lukewarm coffee. She had scattered papers across the table. Now they were bundled together. She lined up the edges and got down to business. She picked up the first sheet from the heap and ran a finger along the border as she read each word. Laying it face down to create a pile beside the original one, she studied the next document. She pulled a pencil out of her pocket and circled a phrase at the bottom of the page. She started a new stack on the left and worked until she had gone through everything.

The files on the right side were of no use to them. She picked up the other sheets and thought of the possibilities.

The noise of the door slamming shut startled her. Scottie watched the couple as they crossed the room and headed to a booth. She glanced at her watch and shifted back to her thoughts. Gibson should be along shortly so she spent the time reviewing a particular paper more thoroughly. She believed this played a crucial part in exposing the truth.

When her cell trilled, she checked the screen for a message. It was Gunner. He was en route with the requested order. The waitress inched closer with a hot steaming pot of coffee. She hoisted it in a gesture that suggested a refresh. Scottie offered her a lopsided smirk. The waitress topped up her mug, cleared away the plates and proceeded to the next table.

Scottie placed the document back on the table. She added cream and sugar to her mug and stirred mindlessly. A violent gust of wind swept up the street and rattled the door. Gibson blew into the room, hanging tightly to the knob. His hair whipped around his face. Crunchy leaves scurried over the ground and tumbled in after him. The restaurant patrons returned to their conversations when it banged shut. He gave a slight tip of his chin and strolled over to her. The table squeezed into the corner made getting in and out tricky. He pushed it around and plunked down heavily, causing the wooden chair to protest with a loud creak. The waitress was on the ball and hurried over with coffee. He ordered a sandwich, lamenting the luncheon at the university he was missing. Scottie passed him a document with the most notable item highlighted. He took a quick look and nodded in agreement. But being the thorough man that he was, he scanned through the whole lot himself—the brochures, the application forms and Robbie's notes. His eyes flashed. The papers corroborated what he had discovered at Royal Roads College.

Gibson looked up. The café was full. There were businessmen in their grey suits, students with their cells and young women gossiping. The chatter and laughter rose and subsided in waves. He produced a blue folder the assistant had compiled for him. Scottie opened the binder and skimmed through the photocopies. The pages were stapled together efficiently and contained all the material needed to apply pressure on the suspect. It satisfied both of the detectives. They ordered more coffee, inclined their heads in partnership and completed their strategy.

"Now we have a motive. Compelling motivation but no proof he killed Robbie," Gibson said. His eyes stuck on a picture behind Scottie's head. An eagle swooping down on its prey. His cell chirped, and he answered sharply.

"Gibson."

"What's going on?" the chief barked down the line.

Gibson told him the sequence of developments that had brought them here.

"I told you to follow the money."

Gibson muttered something about the right course of action. It wasn't only about money. It was more. But he listened as Rex rambled on.

"It fits the facts. Opportunity and motive."

"The Crown Attorney is with us," Gibson said.

"Get the proof," he retorted in a huffy voice and cut off the call.

The veins on Gibson's neck pulsated. He was disconnected from everything except for the pounding of his heart. Another blast of chilly air whistled into the cozy café when the door opened once again. Gunner hurried across the room, a sealed envelope in his hand—the search warrant.

"This is it." Gibson twisted to Scottie.

Feeling renewed, they surged out of their chairs and hastened out. The wind was sharp and unpredictable, churning in all directions. Gibson and Scottie hopped into the F150 ready to rumble. Gunner walked away dejected.

His lips twitched. The fire in his eyes doused. He wandered to his vehicle and regarded the detectives with wispy envy.

"Meet us there," Gibson shouted out after the constable.

A modest grin pulled at the corner of Gunner's mouth, and he flung his hand skyward in acknowledgement. He picked up the pace keen to be involved in the takedown. By the time he got to his vehicle, he was running.

"Gunner has turned into a likeable guy." Gibson showed a self-satisfied smirk.

Chapter 31

Scottie tore up gravel as she pulled into the entrance of the maintenance yard. Gunner jerked to a halt behind her, almost tapping her back bumper.

Na stood near the closed doors, a breath of vapour escaping his lips, gently chattering teeth and a red nose hiding under his upturned collar. With each gust of wind, more heat whisked away from his half-frozen body. Undeterred by the discomfort, he remained at his post watching as Gibson and Scottie stepped out of the F150. Crime scene officer Raymond emerged from around the corner—lanky in his classic suit, a case in hand—and joined the pack.

Scottie flipped Na a salute. Gunner jabbed him on the shoulder showing a bond of friendship between them. Gibson nodded in approval. Na stood up taller and prouder, pleased that the inspector had acknowledged his dependability. Scottie shoved open the door. They followed her as she marched up to the second floor. Only Na remained at the bottom of the stairs, combating the cold outside and scanning the courtyard for trouble.

Scottie rapped on the door frame with her knuckles. Jason peered over his laptop and locked eyes with the intruder—cop eyes, hard and unwavering.

"Can I help you?" He flicked a glance at the others crowding in the doorway.

Three large, menacing bodies squeezed through the opening and invaded his space.

"What's going on?" Jason demanded. His hands bunched into fists.

No reply.

Scottie and Raymond moved along the wall and waited for their part in the take down. Gunner stayed in the hallway to guard the door. He took a power stance, holding one wrist with the other palm and legs spread apart. It would be hard to get past him. Gibson closed his fingers around the door knob and pulled it shut. The latch bolt clicked with a snap as it hit home. The well-oiled team was in position.

Jason curled his lips and snorted an arrogant laugh. He settled back in his chair with an exaggerated casualness. He figured they were up to some shenanigans, nothing that worried him. It was a game he knew fully, and he was willing to play along.

Gibson parked himself on a well-worn seat, wiggling into the cushion. He reached into his upper pocket and flashed an envelope.

"We have a search warrant for your office," he said with no preamble.

"What!" The blow knocked every wisp of air from Jason's lungs along with the conceited look on his face. Trepidation replaced it. The sneer that was prominent moments before had vanished. He averted his eyes and rubbed his cheek, biding his time.

Gibson could almost hear the little wheels spinning. This had been an unexpected action on their part.

"You have no right to come in here waving ill-gotten warrants," he said.

"Robbie knew."

"Knew what?" His voice was petulant and sanguine.

"That you're a phoney." Gibson was sick of mincing words.

Gibson turned to his partner and flicked his wrist toward the notice boards. With one giant stride, Scottie reached the target. Her stony expression gave no clues to her intent. But Jason understood quite clearly what the next move would be. He sucked in his breath to ward off the inescapable.

Scottie grabbed the metal frame and loosened the hold-downs. She drew out the diploma in a slow, deliberate motion. She shoved it toward Jason.

"It's a fake." The stillness in the room was complete.

A squeal of casters rolling along the rutted linoleum broke the silence. Just as quickly, the hush returned as Jason checked his backward shuffle—the last of the smugness wiped from his face. His eyelids drooped and his lips quivered. Almost defeat.

"There isn't a business program at Royal Roads College. Never has been," Gibson said. "Robbie found out. He threatened to expose you. Didn't he?"

"When Robbie got back from the conference last year, he was zealous to upgrade," Scottie interjected, to keep the dialogue going. "We have documents that show us that."

"That's right. Robbie looked at your diplomas and thought he should follow suit," Gibson said. "Why not? You had done well for yourself. Maybe he could do the same."

"Imagine the shock when Robbie recognized what he had stumbled upon. Your deceit," Scottie added.

Gibson stared over the desk. There was a mad glimmer in his usually kind eyes.

Jason dropped his chin on his chest. The once rosy, controlled features had changed steadily to haggard and drawn. He stared at the other certificates hanging staunchly, ones he had earned rightfully but held no meaning. Just a few day-seminars. A light sparked in his flat eyes, and a shade of self-importance crept into his expression. With a moment to connive, he had regained his cool as cheats and liars do.

"So what? I don't know anything about Robbie and his school thing. Even if my diploma is fake, it doesn't mean I killed anybody." He challenged them with his logic.

Although Gibson had hoped for an admission, he knew this was Jason's pawn takes bishop move. It had been a long shot at best. Jason had a large ego and could not be cowed that easily. He needed to misdirect until they turned up the evidence that would convict. All he had was a paper trail to subterfuge not murder. He pressed on with his bluff.

"A witness saw you in your work truck on the boulevard minutes before Robbie was killed," Gibson said effortlessly. He hunched forward and added, "You don't have an alibi."

"I do. I was at the coffee shop."

"You left there with plenty of time to kill Robbie."

His charcoal eyes steeled against Jason's unsteady glare.

"Intent and opportunity," Gibson said. A sharpness in his voice could cut.

"You tried to silence witnesses that saw you," Scottie said. That wasn't true, but it sounded good. The beating of the homeless guy was a different matter. Probably not the dog walker either. That was an errant driver. Just a twist of the knife.

"And AJ getting whacked," Gibson said. He shook with fury convinced that was indubitably on Jason.

"Is that all you have?" Jason chuckled heartily and kicked out his legs. "Where is this evidence?"

Gibson's anger burned deep. He flung open the door and motioned Gunner into the already jammed space.

"Take him downtown for questioning," he barked. He stomped out of the stuffy room like an enraged wildcat, a hiss that started deep in his throat. He would beat this guy somehow.

"You can't do this to me."

The cuffs were cold and heavy. Gunner slapped them on Jason's slender wrists and gave a little rattle. He touched the foreman's elbow to steer him away. Jason yanked from his grip, ran down the stairs and jumped into the police vehicle on his own. He slumped into the lumpy seat and was lost behind blackened glass and a metal barrier. The siren jolted him out of his skin into a kind of panicky reality.

The commotion had brought the workers outside, loosely huddled together on the same spot as before—when this had all started. David frantically stabbed at the buttons on his cell. Tim bounced on his feet, stretching his neck toward the conflict. Nick had his eyes closed, head inclined on the cold steel wall. AJ blew rings in the air. The smoke floated up in perfect circles then dissipated into nothingness. Tony remained in the shop doorway, wide-legged stance, bared teeth and fear in his thoughts.

Raymond began his search of Jason's office.

"Grab the laptop," Scottie called over her shoulder as an afterthought, racing down the stairs.

A loss of status and reputation were powerful motives. Not money, but it translated into money. They had forty-eight hours to unearth the proof. Scottie would be working overtime.

* * *

Numerous vehicles lined the verge of the remote lane by the time Gibson peeled round the corner to his house—a convincing sign that a party was in full swing. He dragged his weary body out of the truck and listened to the wails of laughter spilling out of the residence. In the few flashes of tranquillity between the vivacity, he could pick up the lapping of waves coaxing him toward the bay. The moon hovered directly above the ocean, mimicking its likeness in the still black water. The onshore breeze pushed its path through the trees bordering the seashore, striking his unprotected face with gentle frosty puffs. Gibson sucked in the vigor. His breath whistled out as steam. Although the wind had diminished to an eerie hush, the turmoil in his mind was tumbling with gale force. On the trip home, he had second-guessed his choice to hold Jason before they had concrete evidence. He needed to set aside his qualms, to trust himself and his squad.

Gibson stood motionless for one further moment, drawing in his strength. He had foreseen an evening of wine, dinner and sex. Not to be. So instead, he planted a huge smile on his face and opened the door to the gaiety within. It was Katherine's stage.

"Gibson's here," shrieked a rather tipsy Heather as a rush of chilly air flowed into the opening.

Small pockets of friends stood or sat chattering. Laughter rang throughout the house. A crush of bodies was clustered around the dining table, loaded with trays of finger food and bottles of wine. Gibson observed they had already consumed a substantial measure, so he treated himself to a Pinot Noir. He moved cautiously so as not to spill the generous glass he had poured.

Katherine remained in the centre of the living room—a singular figure—surrounded by her friends. She looked fabulous with soft sable locks tumbling over her naked shoulders and down the open back of her dress. She had whirled around at his return. Her impassioned eyes crackled with a naughty gleam. Gibson drifted closer, took both her hands and kissed inside one palm and then the other. He drew her to him. His lips nibbled her ear, titillating the lobe with his tongue, causing the delicate downy hair on her neck to rise.

The sudden upsurge of cheering permeated the room and shattered the spell. Katherine unravelled herself from the embrace and granted a princess-like curtsey.

Gibson fumbled in his pocket for the gift and placed it in her hand. Katherine squealed. She released the bow with a tug and peeked inside. A gold vintage locket, diamond and emerald encrusted, was nestled in a glass box. The strings of her soul played a tender melody. Her friends pushed forward to catch a glimpse of the treasure.

Gibson moved away to quell the ravenous hunger that had struck him. He filled a china plate and found a spot on the couch. The warmth of the fire washed over him in soothing waves, but his mind was in battle with the day's events. He urged his worries aside with effort and sought to enjoy the amiable company. Soon the evening wound down. The cheerful crowd filtered out to a shroud of icy twilight.

The empty house seemed full—of affection, of contentment. They cuddled on the couch. Katherine leaned in tighter, set a finger to his mouth and said goodnight. He puckered his lips and blew a smooch. She surrendered him to his contemplations.

Gibson slouched further into the cushions and chewed over his actions. His heart softened to a steady pulse. His eyes fluttered closed. He yanked himself up and headed off to bed. Although he was exhausted, sleep did not materialize. He rested on his back and stared at the ceiling. Silvery beams streamed through the crack in the shutters and drifted in erratic patterns across the bedspread. Beside him, the soft and rhythmic breathing of his spouse was tranquil. He counted sheep to impede the internal conversation and to dodge his uncertainties. Soon he was fast asleep.

Chapter 32

"Jason lawyered up," Scottie repeated, sensing that Gibson wasn't listening. She searched for some response, even a twitch, but got nothing. She continued anyway and reported, "He won't talk."

She sat in front of the desk and stretched out her long legs. After several tries to gain feedback from her partner, she became reticent and closed her eyes. Her long flowing lashes brushed her cheekbones.

Gibson stared at the cruise ship docking, giving the appearance of paying no attention. But he was. They had an abundance of material, but they lacked one crucial piece. He struggled to sort it out, to establish the order of events. Storm clouds amassed in the distance. He changed from his position at the window and fled to his desk. He sagged back into his chair and tapped a pen on his thigh.

A smart rap at the door startled both detectives from their contemplation. Gunner stood with a handful of sheets clenched in his hand.

"These might help."

"What have you learned?" Gibson pointed to the vacant chair.

Gunner perched on the edge of the seat and leaned forward. It thrilled him to be part of the investigation. His body vibrated with an energy he had never felt before. He placed the documents in two piles on the desk so they could be viewed easily.

"I've been studying the bank statements since I received them yesterday," Gunner said. He drew gasps of air almost to the point of hyperventilating.

Gibson looked at him in alarm.

His breathing steadied and returned to normal. The episode had blanched his complexion, but he ignored his discomfort and carried on.

"This is Jason's account." He pointed to the highlighted figures on the document in the right stack. "This is a withdrawal of two hundred dollars cash." He underscored the relevance by tapping it with his pencil. "Each month for the previous year."

Gibson remained quiet and waited for him to go on. Gunner touched the second pile with his index finger. A flush snaked up his neck and reached the tip of his ears as he struggled to keep his emotions in check—to stop the rush of words.

"This is Robbie's account. The same. Month, day and amount."

"What happened last December?" Gibson asked. "Assuming Jason was giving Robbie money…maybe these figures are a coincidence." He looked at the date on the bottom of the sheet. He felt gun shy and was extra vigilant about drawing inferences from alternate facts these days. Originally, he had decided it was a hate scandal. And it wasn't. Then he had considered it could be a crime of passion. Another error. There would be no further conjectures.

"Blackmail?" Scottie said with less caution.

"Maybe. Or paying back a loan. We know that Robbie was impulsive."

"We could ask Ellen," Gunner said.

"Good idea."

The detectives headed over to Cadboro Bay, leaving Gunner behind to delve further. The traffic was heavy with shoppers out in full force. They weaved their way past the malls to Henderson Road. Scottie pulled to the curb and parked the vehicle. No children were playing on the grass. Death changed everything. Gibson knocked on the door. They stood on the porch without talking, waiting for someone to answer. Before he could tap anew, the door swung open. Ellen clutched her bathrobe with one hand and tugged at her hair with the other. She frowned and turned away. They followed her inside. She slogged down the hallway. There was still no aroma of cinnamon. The kitchen was lifeless. A stink of stale coffee and sour food lingered. She crumpled into the chair that she had abandoned moments before. A stained place mat, a half-drunk beverage and a plate with dried-out bread crust languished on the table in front of her.

"May I?" Gibson asked as he approached a bench that had been thrust into the periphery of the room. A slow nod gave him consent. He dragged it over and sat down. Scottie stayed at the entrance with notepad and pen by her side. Something—grief—had left the once pristine kitchen to its own devices: filthy dishes on the countertop, a towel on the floor, dust bunnies in the corners and spilled food on the stove top. But no trace of Lily. No fruity cereal or milk cups. It was best not to inquire about the kids.

"We discovered application forms in Robbie's locker," he said. "Was he going back to school?"

A twinge of a smile flickered across Ellen's mouth. She gazed up from her hands resting in her lap. "He wanted a business diploma. To get a better position." She shifted her feet. Restlessness had made her body twitch.

"When was this?"

"Last November when he returned from a conference." Her eyes filled but she bit her lip to stop the pain.

"He didn't go through with it. What changed his mind?"

"I'm not sure. But he mentioned it again lately," Ellen said. "He was ready to do it now."

"Did Robbie lend money to anybody?" Gibson changed tacks.

"Heavens, no," Ellen said. "We could hardly keep our heads above water."

"What about the presents he bought?"

"That's exactly my point. He was overspending, not handing the stuff out. There was just the small sum he gave to Jeff to help him out. That's all." Ellen exhaled heavily.

Gibson stood up. There was nothing else to ask. The accounts were inconclusive evidence of any wrong doing. Another dead end. They needed more. He looked into the living room as they were leaving, but Lily wasn't there.

The ride into town was a battle with heavy traffic and impatient drivers. Scottie parked on the curb across the street from the VIIMCU building. The glass door had a sheen of frost on the outside. Cold air meeting hot. Gibson swung open the door to an empty foyer. The receptionist wasn't around again. He felt dragged out today, and the stairs looked insurmountable so they took the elevator to the second floor. In his office, they picked up where they had started that day. He sat at his desk with his feet splayed out in front of him. Scottie dropped into the chair she had left behind that morning—was it only this morning?—and stretched out. With their positions resumed, they slipped back into their musing until the phone rang.

"Gibson."

He bolted upright. The pencil he had been drumming on his thigh was now furiously flying across a scrap of paper. His scribble was barely decipherable. Sensing a renewed excitement, Scottie bent over to have a snoop. All she saw were squiggly lines.

He hung up and brandished the scrawled note in front of her nose.

"What's that?"

"Proof." Gibson rose his eyebrows. "Raymond found a jacket in Jason's locker with blood on the lining."

"What?"

Gibson repeated what Jocko had just told him.

"The CSI didn't find anything in Jason's office that was of value to us. But he was ticked off that he couldn't get into the locker. He kept on searching and found the key taped in place under a lower drawer of the desk. He brought the jacket to Jocko right away."

"And?"

"This jacket has Jason's initials on the collar and Robbie's blood on the lining."

"Huh?" Scottie wore a puzzled look, not getting the implications. "How does that help? Don't we already have a bloodied jacket?"

"This is a different one." Gibson smiled. "Jocko did an analysis of the dried spots. He said the blood transferred from the jacket you found in the shop—that was Robbie's jacket—to the lining in Jason's jacket."

"What? Could you go slower?" Scottie scratched her throbbing temple.

"Jason wore Robbie's jacket when he killed him." Gibson let Scottie understand this first part and continued. "Blood had splattered on the front so Jason had to stash it somewhere. He ran up the stairs to his office and stuffed the jacket into his locker."

"Underneath his own jacket," Scottie said.

"Right. Then he ran down the back stairs to the parking lot. He came up behind the guys standing at the door and pretended he had just gotten to work."

"Okay, I get that. So now Jason has to get rid of the jacket from his locker."

"That's right. When he tried to ditch Robbie's jacket, he was interrupted. The best he could do was leave it on a hook in the shop. Go back for it later."

"AJ." Finally, Scottie got it.

"I guess Jason thought AJ saw him put the jacket there. Who knows what Jason was thinking? Was he going to kill AJ as well?" Gibson shrugged.

"That's crazy."

"But no matter, you found the jacket before he could get it back."

Scottie beamed her Cheshire cat grin.

"Obviously Jason didn't realize blood had seeped onto the lining of his own coat or he would have dumped that one too."

"I can see Jason champing at the bit." She puckered her lips to whistle a tune and then stopped herself. "Luckily AJ wasn't killed."

"They found bloodied strands of Robbie's hair as well." Gibson smirked. "Too bad." He drew a check-mark in the air.

"Blackmail."

Gibson sat back in his chair to think but didn't reply.

"So. Blackmail?" Scottie spoke again like a broken record. "Robbie realized the diploma was a fake and asked Jason for money. He promised not to expose him, but Jason got jumpy and killed him when it got to be too much for him."

"Yeah," Gibson said.

"Robbie made a poor choice. He should have reported the issue instead. Now he's dead."

"Still comes down to bullying. Jason has been just another bully at the maintenance yard," he said. "You know in that atmosphere the whistleblower usually pays the price."

"What do you mean?" Scottie asked.

"Robbie may have felt that snitching on Jason would land up biting him in the butt. That happens a lot. You wouldn't think it worked that way but it does."

"I've heard that."

"Greed played a part in Robbie's decision too," Gibson said. "Let's go to the lockup and read Jason his rights."

Scottie gave him a fist tap and off they went.

* * *

Jason had been moved to the RCMP station and had been in custody overnight. They entered a room that was a shade of grey that matched the prisoner's eyes. The door clanged behind them with a force that sucked the last of the air out of the room, leaving a stench of sweat.

Gibson was expecting handcuffs to be holding Jason's hands together, but he had them clasped in his lap unfettered. His knuckles were white and his face paled. His eyes darted around the room as if each thought he had was more worrying than the last. The bravado was gone. Gibson planned to use this crack of apprehension to his advantage.

Jason's lawyer had arrived earlier to speak with him. Now Glen remained quietly beside his client with a notebook on the scarred furniture, his finger tracing someone's name carved in the wood. He flicked a lock of hair off his forehead. The stern look on his face looked cemented on.

Gibson placed a document on the table. He spun the paper around so the writing faced Jason and his lawyer. He shoved it along the surface. Jason kept his hands—turning to fists—in his lap. Glen reached for the sheet, but Jason slammed his palm on top.

"Never mind. It's over," Jason shouted. His voice was grating like fingernails on a chalkboard.

"This lab report proves the blood on your jacket is Robbie's," Gibson said. "And hair too." He crinkled his nose at the whiff of something unpleasant.

"Don't say anything," Glen advised. He applied a grip on his client's arm. Jason pushed it aside with a jerk.

"Doesn't matter anymore," Jason said. He looked at the grey walls.

The lawyer shrugged and slumped in his seat.

"I arrived early to confront Robbie about forcing money from me. He shoved me against the wall and jammed his elbow into my throat. I could hardly breath. He was laughing. I got free and grabbed the bat. It was self-defence—"

"Robbie's jacket!"

"What?"

Gibson's charcoal irises went dark and smoky. His thoughts drifted to reasonable murder—if there was such a thing, he would have killed Katherine's ex for all the damage he had done. He rubbed the crook in his nose—not caused by a bar brawl but in a fight with Arthur—and knew he could have stepped over that invisible line just as Jason had. But he didn't.

"You put on Robbie's jacket before he got there."

"Premeditation," Scottie said.

"Don't say another thing."

Jason jumped up and knocked over the frail metal chair. It clanged on the cement floor.

Chapter 33

The drive back to VIIMCU was short. Even the late-night shoppers had finished long ago. Gibson stared out the passenger window, his thoughts lost in the purr of the tires. The moon cast a golden sheen over the landscape. He watched it disappear behind a nebulous mist. In the distance, the mass of clouds had vanished. The sky had darkened from sapphire blue to midnight black. His cell chirped.

"Gibson."

"Good job," Rex thundered down the line.

"Thanks."

Rex rambled on with Gibson barely listening.

A buzz in his ear startled him. The chief had hung up.

Scottie stopped in the 'no parking' zone in front of their building. They let themselves in with an electronic key and dashed up the stairs—elation giving them one last spurt of push. Gibson called the Crown Attorney, but he didn't get an answer so he left a message. They wrote up the final report hunched over the desk in Gibson's office. The air was thick with the smell of burnt coffee from a machine in the far corner. One that was rarely used except for these nights. The lights from the docks blazed through the large window casting long shadows on the floor. A blues radio station played in the background and stopped them from falling asleep. The ceiling lights flickered as if they were tired as well. Soft scurrying of tiny feet resonated down the empty corridor. Scottie stifled a yawn.

"Even the mice are rushing home." Her laughter turned into an episode of hiccups, halting her speech as she tried to recover.

"Let's go."

Back out on the street, the detectives did a fist tap. Scottie drove away, tooting her horn as she took off. Gibson hopped into his truck and made a beeline for Brentwood Bay. As he cruised down the highway, he opened his window. A breeze blew off the ocean and over the peninsula. He inhaled the pure air.

Gibson parked in the driveway and glanced around as he often did when he got home. A minute grin played over his worn features. He could taste the ocean salt on his lips. He let out a single sob and wiped his face with the back of his hand before anybody could notice. Was the salt from the sea or from the tears hiding behind his charcoal eyes? Gibson released a weak chuckle and bounded up the stairs—he thought he had spent all his energy.

The door swung open to a burst of warmth and the aroma of baked bread. He followed his snout down the hallway to the spices and a murmur of voices. Katherine's velvety contralto stood out among them. When he walked into the kitchen, two friends were seated at the table. His wife hovered by the stove stirring a pot.

"Rosemary?" he asked, inhaling deeply, his mouth watering.

"Yes. Heather and I are collaborating on some recipes. With my greenhouse herbs."

Katherine brushed by him—fingers grazed, a fleeting glance—and swept over to the counter. A generous slice of bread with jam and a hot pour of coffee was placed at the head of the table. Gibson plunked down and felt his muscles unwind instantly. He held the present company responsible.

"Delicious." Andrew's empty plate was witness to his remark.

Three eager faces waited for the story.

Gibson took a few swallows and nibbled slowly to savour the herbal flavour. Andrew jabbed him in the ribs to prod him along. Gibson gave a discreet cough. His eyes sparkled. He didn't speak. Not even a glance over.

They stared harder.

"There were many motives but nothing fit," Gibson said. "When Katherine reached for her diploma it twigged." He pointed to the side of his temple. "There it was. The link I was looking for. Robbie and Jason."

As he explained the events in detail, his wife looked intently into his bleary-eyed face. She wondered if her problems had encroached upon her husband. Gibson recognized her worries and gave an imperceptible signal. She smiled. It had been his past misgivings that were distracting, not Katherine's.

"All the innuendos and gossip about Robbie being gay weren't true. That sent us running in circles trying to grab our tails. And Nick with the secret he was keeping from his wife and his buddy, Tim. Oh boy. We thought Nick was guilty, but he was just hiding from himself. There was no affair with Robbie, but…"

Gibson caught his breath and stole a glance toward Andrew.

"The fight David heard was about seniority." He stopped. "Did I leave anything out?"

"I'm glad you guys know about my gay inclination," Andrew said.

Heather let out a low exclamation. Her hair swooshed as she swung her head to peer at Andrew. Finally, she understood why the attempts to attract him had failed.

"Would you like a rose garden? A fresh dawn for your new life." Gibson grabbed his wife's hand and squeezed hard. Katherine was a soul that could soar. Her gold locket twinkled in the light.

He hoped the panic attacks would cease. If not wholly, at least a road to happiness could be found. His eyelids flickered—with good expectations or with drowsiness? Gibson knew tomorrow would be a brilliant day for a kayak adventure.

If you enjoyed this book, please let others know by leaving a quick review on Amazon. Also, if you spot anything untoward in the paperback, get in touch. We strive for the best quality and appreciate reader feedback.

editor@thebookfolks.comE

All titles by Kathy Garthwaite

In this series:

MURDER ON VANCOUVER ISLAND
MURDER AT LAKE ONTARIO
MURDER ON THE SAANICH PENINSULA

In the Detective Flint series:

THE ALLEY
THE STUDY

Why not try the other books in the series?

The veteran detective is flown out to the east of the country to help set up a major crimes task force. He soon has a murder on his hands when a local shopkeeper is found dead on the beach. Estranged from his melancholic wife, Gibson's loyalties become divided.

When a woman is murdered, Inspector William Gibson immediately suspects her husband is responsible. His junior partner is not so sure. But when the truth emerges it has a knock-on effect that will change the detective's life for ever. And not in a good way.

Sign up to our mailing list to find out about new releases and special offers!

www.thebookfolks.com

Manufactured by Amazon.ca
Bolton, ON